My Complicated Destiny

Swarali Wankhade

Invincible Publishers

First published in India in 2016 by Invincible Publishers

ISBN: 978-93-86148-28-5

Invincible Publishers
G-120, Sushant Lok III, Hong Kong Bazar Lane Sector 57, Gurgaon-122002

Opposite Kasturba Ashram, Radaur Distt Yamuna Nagar, Haryana- 135133
Digitally Printed at Replika Press Pvt. Ltd.

About the author

* * *

My debut novel 'My Complicated Destiny' marks an important happening event in my life, released on my 21st birthday adding the essence of a beautiful gift of imagination and putting that as an art of writing where words express feelings.

Being born and raised in Hyderabad, blessed to have a lovely family. Though graduated as a computer science engineer, I hate computers. Pen and books are my dear friends.

All words collaborated in "MCD" are truly from my heart. Words and emotions framed a different picture in mind hence, putting all that on paper only when I am upset. Therefore fortunately the journey of MCD began on its own.

As an author, my attempt was to weave the concept of unconditional love and respect in every relationship since we are not aware about tomorrow.

Acknowledgement

* * *

My Complicated Destiny wouldn't have been possible without the support of few important and special people in my journey.

A very big thanks to my parents Sanjeev Kumar and Bhavana Wankhade for showering unconditional love and support throughout my growing years.

I would like to thank Mr. Ajay Setia for being my mentor, guide and newly found friend. My editor Malvika Solanki for being so patient and my designer Sneha Agarwal and Ravi for actually putting my imagination into a crystal clear picture on the cover. A big thank you to the entire team of Invincible Publishers.

A heartiest thanks to all my siblings Anmol Wankhade, Dolly Wankhade, Harshavardhan Wankhade, Sankalp Jadhav and my dearest pet Moti. Thanks for all your love.

Lastly, my best friends for being in my life Venkat Krishnan and Danush. No matter how much ever we fight, we gonna be best friends forever.

Prologue

* * *

In my small world, you came uninvited...

Lightened my empty world and changed things around...

I kept thinking the reason for my life.

But the answer is still hidden as I know the fact… believe things change as per time, season, and the person in fact.

But I believe you'll remain the same as the apple of my eye.

I wanted a person with no name, no face, just a soul whom I could trust a lot.

But not fall in love with a heavy heart…

Then the face appear out of the blue, making me blush…

Things tend to look all good andnew.

Now I am scared of the change.

Love it at the same time a lot….

Now days and weeks and years pass by… As you know, I will be no more alive…

WILL YOU LOVE ME? IS WHAT I WANT TO ASK.

Reading this letter, tears dwell in his eyes.

Chapter one
United states:

* * *

UNITED STATES:

The flight landed and as he stepped out, the atmosphere, the cold breeze and at a far distance he could see the sky and earth meeting at the horizon. He felt happy as he always wanted to be here. But he felt so lonely at the same time. He is among strangers wondering how he would survive. Missing Nishk was something he would never let off his mind. He took a cab and reached his hostel. He looked at the tall building in front of him with well-designed exterior, entered the lift and pressed no. 27, stood in front of room no 2706 and found the door to be unlocked and was sure he had to share his room with someone else. He knocked, being always disciplined. An American guy opened the door and greeted him warmly as if he was waiting for him. He walked slowly and looked around, scanning every corner of the room. It was indeed beautifully furnished.

'Hello, Jake', He said and extended his hand.

'Hello, Zed Oberoi', he shook back.

Nice to meet you, they both said at once.

Laughed.

"I knew I would be sharing a room with an Indian", Jake said.

"Oh so, is there anyone else gonna join us, or just two of us??"

"Micheal Lithoper from Germany", Jake said.

He occupied the vacant bed, placed his suitcase on the other side and took out his clothes.

I'll shower first and then I l unpack my bag, Zed said and headed towards the restroom which was quite big. As soon as the cold water hit his body, he felt so relaxed and refreshed.

Zed came back and started unpacking. Of three beds, Jake choose the very first one and there was a wardrobe adjacent to every bed, study table, a common shelf, the room was fitted with two a/c's, and an LED TV hanging on the wall and a balcony from where the view is just awesome. The highway, the tall buildings, greenery till few miles away, the beech, sand and water shone like diamonds from a distance. He inhaled the fresh breath and closed his eyes savoring the moment.

Jake fell on Zed's bed as he was unpacking. Jake is a very kind person, tall and had almond shaped green eyes, skin so pink that all the green nerves beneath could clearly be seen, very friendly and well mannered. Zed guessed that he also would be good at academics.

He pulled out a box of sweets from his suitcase and the smell attracted Jake.

"What's that dude?" Jake asked.

"Indian deserts!!" He said and offered him.

He took one and "uummmm…lovely", he said.

Zed gave the complete box to Jake.

"Love you dude..", he winked back.

Zed neatly arranged his clothes in his closet while Jake kept talking about his family, friends and his beloved girlfriend. "She is in California and I am here, I miss her dude". He said starring at her pic.

Memories of Nishk struck his mind all of sudden when Jake kept talking about his girlfriend and how much he missed his parents too. A weak smile was plastered on his face

"I am hungry", Zed said.

"Let's go to cafeteria", he suggested.

"Sounds good" and they left the room.

Jake ordered something and for Zed. It was even difficult to pronounce the name of the dish.

He was just waiting for his order and hoped it is edible at least. The waiter served and all he could see was leafs and raw veggies stuffed with two large buns, with extra cheese. He took a bite and made faces.

Jake could clearly read the disappointment on his face and he apologized.

"It's Ok".

"No wait a sec", he said and went to the counter again.

He didn't know, what Jake was doing there. Zed saw him talking about something and he kept doodling with fork on his plate.

"Would you like to have a" he took long pause. He could not read and simply ordered.

Zed smiled at his plight. There was an Indian counter thankfully. He wished at least this time it would be edible for Pete's sake.

They walked around the campus. Jake introduced him to few of his friends who were good to hangout, he felt at the moment. The day was complete and they walked back to the room and saw a guy, stylish beard, tall, muscular physic.

Jake greeted.

But he ignored and slept on his bed. Jake stared

at Zed and shrugged his shoulders. Jake too jumped on his bed and quickly fell asleep. He opened his laptop and wrote an e-mail to Nishk. He typed the entire story about what had happened; about Jake and his place but could not send it as he remembered no contacts and nothing. He closed his laptop and lay down on the bed.

Chapter Two

* * *

Next day started with great enthusiasm. He had early morning bath, freshened up, he kissed his parent's photo which he kept at the extreme right on his bed and left the room for college. His only focus was his career and intention was to never make any friends. He was sitting alone on his bench in the middle of the room, surrounded with 120 people around him. They were talking and laughing, some were busy with their laptops and few were staring at him. He felt so awkward but could not help. A minute later Jake joined him and he felt reviled. Jake showed him his girlfriend's photo Autumn, to kill time. She was beautiful.

"Nice", he said.

"I know", He kissed the photo.

The lecture began and it went on for another hour which kept him busy. Since the very first day he got back to his studies. Assignments were given on the very first day itself. He was not able to adjust in the first week and was not sure what to do. Lots of even-odd things wandering in his head. Later he was occupied with so much work, he could hardly make time for fun.

Jake wondered how he could live such a nerd kind life.

Many girls were attracted to Zed, some of them were looking for a chance to talk to him and few even asked his phone number to have hot chats. Jake then suggested him to get an international sim so that he could talk to his family on a regular basis.

Few weeks later he got his number activated, the

moment it was activated, he restlessly dialed Nishk's Number. On the first ring itself he hung up.

All the words oscillated in his mind 'no contacts'. He missed her so much. He would often talk about her to Jake. Guessing what she might be doing at the moment and on and on. He assumed that even she would be missing him.

When ever he would meet any new people, he would never miss the chance to talk about his best friend Nishk. Anyone could hardly understand his feelings but his face lit up even a single mention of Nishk. He missed her every single day.

Weeks, months, passed on and by now Jake and Zed became the best buddies. Zed helped Jake in academics, bunking, home work and also during exams.

Zed was a genius since school days. His interest in designing cars, ideas of having the best design with best machines started since he was 11. He spent hours and sometimes sleepless nights in front of the computer, designing layouts. He would engage himself in learning and researching something new every time which made him grab this scholarship at such a prestigious college and so he decided to become an automobile engineer by profession. Later planned for abroad after seeing the advertisement on TV. He loved his work, the zeal, the passion resemble in his work. He maintained his notes so neatly, his handwriting, running notes and records and the numerous doubts he raised made the professor sick. But everyone liked him. Students raised eyebrows when he asked questions or solved any difficult problems, they found him mysterious and genius.

He topped in his semester exams and the professors were too proud of him. Everyone loved and appreciated to have him in their class. He made a couple of friends with whom he would hang out. He would often accompany Jake to bars and nearby clubs, had fun, tasted wines and champagne at times. He learnt to speak Various languages. He was enjoying his life to the fullest because he promised Nishk he would stay happy. But, he never dated any girl.

In the month of December when it was snowing, he felt very delighted. He always wanted to feel the snow right and sadly it never snowed in India. Though his parents took him to various amusement parks for his love for snow.

He used to educate his friends about Indian culture and festivals as he missed having fun. Jake and others too talk to Zed's parents on Skype. They were happy seeing his pleasant smile and surrounded with kind people. He always wanted to ask about Nishk , but he never did.

On Christmas Eve, Jake's girlfriend surprised him coming all the way from California and entered their room through a window as girls were not allowed into boys hostel. She wore jeans and a hoodie above her head. She was just like the way he had seen in the photo. Fair complexion, aqua colored eyes, blonde hair dyed red at the bottom, lips coated with dark red lipstick. She was actually beautiful. As Jake saw her, his jaw dropped down and took her into his embrace and hugged so tightly and they kissed each right in front of Zed. He stood their astonished but was happy seeing them soo happy. Jake introduced Autumn to Zed and she said "wow Indian!" and smiled beautifully. Jake and Autumn talked so much and would often got cosy, she sat on his lap and Zed was forcefully made to sit with them. She was exactly like Nishk he though in his mind. Yes, same as in talkative. How badly, he had urge to kiss her to shut her mouth, but he never crossed the line. He came out of his thoughts when he heard autumn called his name a bit louder. She asked Zed to accompany them to Christmas eve but he politely denied, let them spend some private time together and decided to stay back and enjoy watching sports or movies. He became die heart fan of soccer after going to the US.

Chapter three

The years passed by ....and by then he became so famous and yes, his best friend Jake too was well known to all. He topped every semester and his layouts were absolute fabulous. He started his projects with senior's right from second year and built extremely fabulous cars with absolute accurate speed and accurately calculating millage. The color, designs made every one turn their head in surprise. People at the campus would die to have a glance at his breath taking invention. He received young scientist award for his invention and various awards for exhibiting his talents at the national level and college level. Many awards were brought to the college and all honor went to his hard work and determination.

The three years were successfully gone by with lots of fun around. He visited all neighboring countries with Jake and others. Sometimes Autumn would accompany them. That's when how badly he wanted Nishk by his side. He would purchase any unique thing during his visit to gift Nishk and his parents and few friends back in India. By then he knew few western festivals and was actively became a part of it such as tomato festival, bull fights and much more. He even got used to the veggies and salad. He taught Autumn how to cook biryani and few spicy dishes as she wanted to be a chef. Eventually, Jake would be happy. Most of the time Autumn would sneak into their room and surprise both of them. Perhaps, this was the secret between the three.

Prof. Johnson Thomas was introduced in their university in their final year. Everybody was excited and gathered in the auditorium. The auditorium was filled with 5000 students of which around 250 toppers were filtered from every branch.

Prof, Johnson Smith was famous, recognized as a philosopher, who had knowledge on every subject. He had come there to deliver lectures and share his knowledge on various subject and the toppers were supposed to ask questions related to their research or project. As Zed was preparing his next layout, he made all the preparations well in advance and with utmost care he prepared the list of questions to be ask in the conference hall. As the event started, right from introduction everything went according to the agenda. The lectures on quantum physics, computer forensic, etc., the professor covered every topic of the stream. As per the instructions, questions were supposed to be asked. The questions raised by Zed at the conference related to his research made the Prof think twice before answering and later by evening, the event came to an end.

Then, the Prof had a private discussion wi the principal, the Dean, head of the departments, secretary. . He came to know about Zed's inventions and his contribution to their college's reputation by winning numerous awards and praised Zed and willingly offered him a job in his multi billionaire company paying the highest package. Zed was happy when he got to know but was not keen on taking up the job in US. He was never after money. After being convinced by his faculty, he signed a contract with prof and hence the deal was finalised. Soon after his graduation, he joined Mr Smith's company. Success was just like a shadow, following him everywhere. The clients all over the globe loved his designs and new inventions and the investors were ready to invest huge amounts with all belief and trust in his work. But he was nowhere concerned about the number of zero's added to his account, he was just waiting for the contract to end although he was happy that he had earned enough and made his parents proud. He would simply count days. The one and only reason, he wanted to leave everything and go back to India, just to meet his love, Kanishka.

Having no contact and spending each day without even talking to her was something too painful for him, but the immature promise and condition put front at him by her. Without any choice, he simply agreed.

Though he was hooked up in many activities, yet he felt alone. The void can be filled only with the magic she hold within her. He would simply look at the calendar each night.

The time sand was empty now and his hard work was paid off and finally decided to leave for India. He gave the last layout of his invention to the prof and was sure the launch of his new designed car would take around 10-11 months and rumors were that his invention would be presented at a big platform later. But he did not care to go in the depths of it. But perhaps, he received his cheque well in advance as the team had enough faith in him and finally he greeted his people before leaving. Though many were disappointed but he was not ready to stay there any longer. He met all his friends one last time, especially Jake and Autumn.

They exchanged a manly hug and Autumn kissed on his cheek and said good bye.

Chapter Four
India

* * *

India:-

He saw his parents at the airport,, his mom was overjoyed as tears rolled down her cheeks. He was so happy and gave a quick hug. His mom complimented him that he has now turned into a handsome hunk. a grown up young man. He was looking around with a hope to see her as he had told his parents about his arrival. But sadly she was not there. His inquisitiveness made him ask them about her but he kept quite as he thought she might surprise him or might do something mischievous. As he reached home, he felt nothing had changed. His house was the same as he left years ago. He went to his room and memories of happy times played in his mind and he smiled like a love stuck teenager. He looked at Nishk's home from his window, but all he saw was a giant lock on the main gate. He sensed something weird.

Later in the evening, he went for a walk and stood in front of her house. On seeing the lock he just looked around. Dry leaves surrounded the garden area where trees once were green and fresh, now just dry like in a desert. Aunt never keeps her house so dirty. He looked up at her window but it only had spider webs over the glass.

He rushed home and quickly asked his parents where is Kanishka., "I had been to her place and looks like no one stays there now". They were lost in thoughts and then looked at each other, trying to recollect about whom he actually was asking and then said, oh! that girl kanishka, the Mathur's right, one week after you left they too moved out to some other place I guess and we have not seen them in years. We have no clue about their Whereabouts. He was shocked to hear that and this came as a blow in his stomach and tears dwelled in his eyes.

He felt so restless that he immediately contacted all his and her friends on Facebook and asked about her but nobody was in contact with her. He recalled that day, at the airport, waving good bye, moving out with Daniel... yes yes it must be Daniel. "He might know about her". He tried somehow find Daniel but couldn't make it. He was fighting back his tears. He felt he had lost everything! He lost all hopes. He slammed his door and kept crying until he fell asleep. This was something unbelievable. All the thought he kept alive, have just dead. His eyes were swollen and puffy when he woke up and again the feelings killed him. He kept dwelling in guilt for actually considering that promise. He walked towards his window and saw her house covered with trees, doors locked, dry leaves all around. The balcony full of dust, where once she used to stand and smile at him and sometimes sneak in his room at mid night whenever she had a small tiff with her mom. When he made his way to her place, the chill air on his cheeks made him feel even worse in the December nights. The tears left their stains on his cheeks with eyes completely swollen. She was his destination and now he knew nothing about her and felt like he had lost all that he gained.

His mom knocked at the door. He assured and

said, "I will be there within 10 minutes".

"Mom, dad, didn't you even try to find out about Nishk and her Mom?" He asked in a serious tone filled with pain and hell lot of questions to be answered. "She made me strong, so strong that I made my way across seven seas alone".

"Reply mom", he said in low husky voice looking straight in her eyes.

"No Zed, we don't know about them. Mrs. Mathur did not even attend any social parties. Many even asked me about her but we were clueless. The house has been just the way it is now. We thought they had left this state or country", Mom said slowly lowering her eyes..

He finally broke down and fell on his knees. His parents were shattered to see their beloved son in such a state and comforted him. And he finally told with all the courage he gathered to tell her instead, "I loved her all these years. I just love her. I just love her. I patiently waited for her all these years with a hope of seeing her once I return. We promised each other. We did. How did this happen." He sobbed.

He didn't know what to do and very slowly nine months simply passed and he could not find her. He was dying every single day. He did not even sketch any design. He would simply lock himself in his room all day long. All his attempts to find her, failed miserably.

One morning he went for a walk and looked at the familiar garden where he used to come finding her when she was sad. It was her favorite place. As he entered there, all of his memories came back. He sat on a bench and was lost in thoughts. Two men stood in front of him. Zed looked at them and a smile crept on his lips. Daniel and Rohit, he shouted in joy. They exchanged hugs and laughed talking recollecting their days back in college. It made him feel better. He actually laughed after months of depression.

Suddenly Daniel asked…

"Did you meet Kanishka?"

The earth swept beneath his feet when he heard Daniel's question.

"No, do you know about her? Mom and dad did not meet them since I left". He asked if they knew where she was. He asked in a fast tone.

Getting back to being restless all again.

"Answer me bro", he said again. Daniel and Rohit looked at each other and they were stealing eye contact.

"Is she alright?" Was the only question that came out of his mouth with tears in his eyes.

Daniel said "I will tell you everything just be calm and sit down.".

Zed was scared to death.

"When we left you at the airport and walked towards the parking, I had to meet someone so I gave keys to Kanishka and asked her to leave alone. She was crying actually, but I did not know what to say. She simply smiled and walked towards the car.

And when we moved in opposite directions, I heard a horrible sound. I turned back and…"

"And what????" Zed asked.

"And I saw her in a pool of blood. An accident. I immediately took her to the hospital and she had severe injuries and was unconscious for almost three days. I don't know after that. I left for Mumbai for studies and your parents know nothing about this because nobody ever told them anything. I tried to contact you but I guess by then your sim card stopped working…"

"Now where is she? And how is aunty?"

"I don't know Zed".

"They had shifted from here, Mom told me!", Zed said.

There was suddenly silence. None knew what to speak.

"I think, we should check in hospital again". Rohit suggested.

"It's been five years and 9 months and I don't think we will get any damn information about her". Zed said in frustration running his fingers through his hair.

Daniel agreed with Zed.

"But still guys, they have records and I think this will help. And which hospital did you take her?", Rohit asked Daniel.

"City hospital", he said.

"I will go and find". Zed said.

"We will also join you". They both said in unison.

"It's my fight, I will get my love back", He said.

"Love???"

"Yes. I love her a lot", he said. Now he tells very proudly to everyone.

They smiled. "But we will also come along" they said and he agreed.

He went back home with a new hope.

Chapter Five
Flash back

* * *

15 years back:

Kanishka's pov:

Kanishka Mathur, extremely beautiful, black waist-length naturally straight hair, brown eyes, soft and awesomely tough. She was beyond imagination and sometimes cocky.

Kanishka's home @ 6:00 pm:

"Mom! I just returned home and please don't irritate me, you know I don't like to be surrounded with all oldies and indulge in these parties either. Overall those silly 40-50 yrs old aunties-type parties. You take me there as always, get involved yourself and leave me behind all alone."

"Mom, are you there? Are you even listening to me? Mom! Mom!" I scream from my room.

"First have something, you must be hungry we can discuss this later". I cut her and said "No more discussion mom" I plead. "Ok fine as you wish honey". Mom came closer and kissed my cheeks. I could not believe what I just heard. I sign with relief. Oh freak! Mom screamed as if she has seen a dragon. "Look at yourself Nishk, look at your hair where is the other ribbon, why are your shoes and skirt so dirty and muddy, did you get into a fight again?"

"Any complaints again this time then I am gonna…", I cut her again. "No mom we had sports and so it became dirty I guess". I grin. "Get freshened up first I have prepared your favorite, burger".

"Wow I will be back shortly".

"Yea hurry up".

After an hour or so Mom came out of her room, in a lovely black saree with red shinny border, a red lipstick, slight makeup, an expensive bracelet around her wrist that dad had gifted her years ago and that's the only thing I remember about dad, her long hair well braided, added to this her fair skin making her look extremely beautiful than usual. I thought to tag along, but I recollected the last time's incident. I was the only girl among all the women. Mom introduced me to some of her friends and I was shared as a chocolate among them, hugs followed by kisses and then pulling my cheeks. I did not like it at all and kept staring at mom all the while ...WHOOO unimaginable. I got back from my thoughts.

"I am leaving honey, I will be back by midnight and please be awake to open the door for me and I hope that your little stomach is satisfied with the sandwich and nanny is on leave and watchman uncle is also off duty and am I forgetting something?" Mom asked herself, and I look astonished at her and then she continued "...in case any monster or ghost comes to gobble you, please do manage it sweetheart, bye." She smiled and opens the door to go out.

I breathe heavily and said "I really wanna come with you I...I... Was just kidding but then you took it damn seriously and wait for 10 more minutes I will get ready". I rushed to my room without even waiting for her reply.

I wore a knee length blue frock and then blue hair band, added to that my blue purse, my blue ear rings, a blue gem ring, a diamond bracelet and of course blue sandals. I checked myself in the mirror and I look perfectly pretty. Then I appeared in front of mom, who was talking over the phone and gave a sarcastic smile looking at me. She ends the call. "What made you change your mind dear?" mom asked and I shrugged, "I did not want to ruin your evening as you looked so sad. Mom drove all the way to party club and car halted there.

As we stepped out of car I told myself "get ready Kani".

Mom and I walked hand-in-hand, she was greeted by many beautiful women all so well dressed up with heavy makeup and too very heavy jewelry. Few were slim, and others were fat, and few were extra-ordinarily fat, and not so surprisingly the same happened again. I was the only kid in the hall, mom was involved in her gathering and I occupied the corner place and gazed everywhere.

All the women usually discuss about jewelry, complaints about their husbands, their past affairs, next vacations, any romance in colony and what not.

Few intolerable minutes passed. Later I saw a women, 5'8 tall, whitish, short hair, light pink lipstick and very slight make-up. She was wearing jeans. She looked completely different from other women in the hall, "may be the new member of this club", I thought. Another woman introduced this lady to everyone and later my mom and that lady were talking like old friends. But they were not even acquaintances. And the next moment my heart was in my throat. I was shell shock. I saw a boy of my age, along with that lady and my mom heading towards me, and I sat still holding the empty straw in my mouth out of glass. Mom introduced me to "Mrs. Meneka Oberoi." I greeted her and she flushes. "Your mom has told me the entire scene that has happened before coming here", she said and I passed angry look at mom. Well to get out of this boredom meet your new friend ZED said Meneka aunty. We exchanged hello, though I was not clear how to pronounce his name. Mom and aunt left us saying "have fun kids" froze and thanked God for showing some mercy. I jumped out in excitement.

'Calm! Calm !' he said.

I slap his back hard and put my arm around his neck and draged him to another corner. He was scared as hell by now.

Zed was a good looking boy, very silent and reserved type of a guy, exactly opposite to me, his hazel eyes, round glasses like that of Harry Potter, well-combed hair, surely his mom might have made it. In fact, he looked studious and he is a valedictorian.

To kill the awkward silence I began "Well what's your name. How to pronounce?" I asked. "It's Z.E.D", in a peculiar staccato voice "ZED OBEROI" he replied. "It's simple" he said. "Oh really?" I try to scare him as to confirm how well I can bully him.

"So Zed your mom bought you here forcefully or you often attend such parties surrounded by women?" I question him teasingly! "NO.. NO..." He defends. Actually dad is out of town and so I was all alone. So I had no choice. "What about you?" he asked. "Same here" I replied in a simple tone. Before he could ask me anything I shot another question "So tell me about your friends." He paused for a while and said "I have no friends". I was amazed by his answer and immediately extended my hand "friends?". He looked stunned. After a gasp he shook his hand and asked "really". I squeezed tightly and said "yes yes yes" thrice. Later left his hand and laughed loudly.

Later we started talking about our favorite color, followed by dish, chocolate, ice cream, pencil, eraser, crayon, sketch, teacher, subjects, place, biscuit, juice, flowers, fruits, comics, paintings... our likes were completely different the only common thing was we loved to watch Disney . Those couple of hours were magical, I found a new friend and he found his only friend. We shared a great bond. Our moms came and Meneka aunty said, "hope you kids had great time" both Zed and I replied "yes" in unison and we all four laughed. See you soon and we left the place.

Next day at school I excitedly told about Zed to all my friends Anna, Bharat, Raj, Yash, Mehek, Rashi. Anna is my best friend. She really cares for me like a sister. She is tall, smart, she has the anglo-indian look like figure and wears a high pony tail. Bharat pretends to be the coolest and has great knowledge about latest fashion and loves to have a collection of shoes. Raj is another cool guy and also short tempered. Usually Raj and Bharat get involved in fight on small issues later get it sorted after entering into the dean's office. Yash, brave is another name for Yash, he would love to breaks all rules and later handles everything as a wise person.

Mehek is other close friend. Grey hair and has a good IQ among all of us and we all are in our fifth standard. I used to share the same bond with everyone but now Zed became my special friend. I spend most of my time with him, which ultimately results my other friend getting angry.

Chapter Six
5 years later:

* * *

Meneka aunty and my mom too became close friends. The Oberio family would visit our place at times for dinner or any other occasions and we were also invited for birthdays, anniversaries and festival events. Both the families were close friends and also neighbor's. Now, that we are in our 10th std, the board exam fear was instilled in us by teachers and parents. So, mom and aunty both had decided to enroll us in the famous tuition academy. I wonder why Zed had to go to tuition when he always gets 95% throughout his academic and I get 70%, quite enough for my satisfaction. Anyway we were forced to attend tuition after school hours.

After reaching home, I called zed and asked "are you ready for party" and I giggled. He replied in shock and worried, "What party? We have to attend tuition Nishk".

"I was just checking your memory stupid. Anyway, call me when you start OK!" and was about to hang up the call.

He replied, "You scared the hell out of me Kani".

"I know you coward", I said and laughed.

"I am not", he said.

"OK coward". I said again.

"Bye" he said and hung the phone on my face.

I usually tease him and call him coward, his face would turn red and would become upset. Later I I'd cajole him and everything gets sorted.

Since, we being neighbor's I could hear Zed's

cycle clink and so I'd peep out of my window and there he would be. This was our usual routine. Today I signaled him and was in front of him after a minute. I said "hi", but then he did not reply. I walk with my cycle and Zed does the same. In fact I follow Zed. I try to figure out what is his problem and the reason for such a strange behavior. "Did anyone smack you?"

"Lemme see your face", I move forward to look at him dramatically. As I raise my hand up to touch his face he shoved me off. Finally after assuming lot of things I get it, it's the "coward thing". Then, he gave me a I-hate-you look and then I get the conformation. I halt my cycle right in the middle of the road and apologize dramatically, he felt so embarrassed as people look at us and he is too shy. He forgives me and I laugh madly till we reach our tuition.

"Our first day", I said and we looked at the apartment and on second floor, our class where an elderly man was teaching Maths, the subject I hate the most and Zed hates to hate the subject. Before entering the class, I warned Zed to sit next to me and he just nodded. The class was partitioned into two equal halves each row for boys and other was for girls. Zed left me alone and sat in boys row and I followed him. Only Zed and I were sitting in the same bench and I was totally OK with it but he was a nerd. I would often pick such games which would drive him crazy. He was mad at me for some unknown reason and upon asking for several times, he still remained stubborn. This ultimately drove me even crazier. "Fine" I said. On our way back home, the road would be crowded and we have to cross two signals. In midway I halt my cycle and looked at him, but he still remained same.

I gave a mischievous smirk and said, "I am closing my eyes and you are going to instruct me. If you are wrong at any point you very well know the consequence", I said.

He gave a puzzled yet scared look and before he could open his mouth I peddled my cycle closing my eyes shut.

"Unbelievable", he said and shouted me to stop. Well I donno where I was heading and this stupid was simply yelling my name.

"Duffer tell me the way else I am gonna die and you would be responsible", I said.

"Wait..." He said.

"Idiot", I said.

"Slow down", he said and I took control of my cycle and slowed down.

"Speed breaker just three cm ahead", he said and

I applied the brakes.

"Look Nishk stop and open your eyes, you are scaring me".

"I know you are coward." I said and laughed out and I am pretty sure people might be looking at us.

"Slow left, put one leg down" he said. I did accordingly.

I could hear the honking on either side of me, so I guess I was in between the moving vehicles.

But I trusted him. He would never make a miss, he may be a nerd but not stupid. He was smarter than anyone I knew so far.

"Side, there is a car coming, and I slowed down, almost stopping but then he said move bit fast the lane is quite clear.

I knew we are in our lane now and I am quite aware of every corner of my colony,

"Park on your right, your home", he said and I parked and opened my eyes.

Zed was standing in front of my eyes, kept his cycle on stand and was about to shout at me but just then I burst out laughing. This time really hard, clutching my stomach tight.

Sweat beads on his forehead...

His face's color changed, he was angry by now but couldn't do much.

I took the helm of my scarf and raised my hand to wipe his face and again he shoved me off.

Usually Zed feels uncomfortable when I hold his hand, or sit beside him, touch him or rest on his shoulder his expression becomes indecipherable.

And so three months passed with lots of fun and pre exams. Finals are in next two weeks.

Chapter Seven

✻ ✻ ✻

One night after dinner, mom and I were discussing about my exams and my future and suddenly she started coughing, later much worse, I ran into kitchen and bought a glass of water.

This was something different, mom is very particular about her health and she regularly gets medical checkup.

"Are you alright??" I asked.

"Yes Nishk, don't worry I am alright", she said and gave me half hug.

I asked her to sleep. She signed and left.

I started studying for my exams but could not concentrate. Mom's such a condition could not be just normal.

I spent sleepless hours and then I heard mom's voice, as if she needed me and at around midnight 2 o clock. I rush to her room and saw her on floor suffering, she was going through some severe pain. I started crying and didn't know what to do and I had Zed's number on my speed dial, I called him and told entire thing in one breath and hung up the phone. Within next five min Zed's entire family arrived and mom was taken to the hospital and was immediately admitted. Several dreadful hours passed and finally doctor called aunty and uncle to his cabin. I am left with Zed and kept crying.

"Look Nishk stop crying. Everything is alright. Just stop crying. You have always been a strong girl and now you have to take care of your mom, just stop crying", he said.

I cried even more burring my face into his shirt and slowly silently calm down. I saw aunty and uncle coming out of cabin, Zed and I stood up and ran to Meneka aunty and asked what happened to mom??

"Your mom is fine. She will talk to you once she gets back from unconscious state". Aunty tries to convince me and it did not execute well and she could read the expression on my face. She took me towards bench and sat there. She took my hand into hers and said "your mom and I went out for coffee the other day. I don't know what made her tell me about her past, the reason for your Mom's and Dad's separation, their divorce" She specifies and since that moment she is been unwell and…" she stopped "...and what aunty?" I asked as a tear rolled down my cheeks. "And now due to over stress she went through a heart attack Nishk". She said and was silent. "I cried silently, then breathed heavily, finally broke down and out of curiosity or love or concern Meneka aunty hugged me and calmed me. I don't know when I fell asleep in her lap.

I was on couch when my eyes opened and mom exactly opposite to me on bed still sleeping and then enters Aunty. "I think you should go home dear, Zed and uncle are waiting for you out", she said.

I saw the clock on the wall it showed 9 'o' clock and I kept staring at mom.

"Nishk", she said again.

"No aunty I can't leave mom all alone", I said in a very low voice.

"I am here don't worry".

"But....".

She cuts me and said, go home have something "Zed will take care of you."

I nodded, she came along till outside the door'.

Uncle, Zed and I got in a car, all the time I held Zed's hand and the car halted in front of his house.

I will take bath and come to have breakfast at your place I said and started walking towards my home.

After taking shower, I sat on the sofa and don't know what was running in my mind, suddenly I heard a knock at door and bluntly asked to come in. It was Zed and he came straight towards me. "Look at your hair, they are still wet" he said and rushed to my room returned with a towel and started toweling my hair as I sat numb lost in thoughts, not a word out from my mouth, he kept on talking something to cheer me and I did not even listen to what he was saying. He held my hand and we both head towards main door and then some electric vibes gushes in me, I pull him towards me and hugged him tightly as if there was no tomorrow, being emotionally weak at that moment I guess I made that move and he was in dead shock. I hugged him even more tightly and babbled something. I could feel his hands around me. Then, there was complete silence. Thin air passing in the room. To break the silence he said. "dad is waiting for us. Lets go" and I followed him.

I did not wish to have breakfast so Roy uncle was feeding me and then the phone rang. He excusesed and kept the plate on table ultimately grabbing the chance Zed took charge of it, I made face at every bite

, he narrows his eyes and stuff the spoonful of food in my mouth. Uncle returned and on seeing my empty plate, "good girl" he said and smiled. "We have to go to hospital now, your mom wants to see you Kani" he says and I jumped out of chair and they followed me.

As I open the door widely, I saw her sitting on bed and Meneka aunty at her side. I walked slowly towards her fighting back my tears and I lost control over and burst into tears. SSSHHHUU I am alright honey, look I am fine stop crying and she kissed me all over my face. Doctor entered the room and we all greeted him and he smiled back .

Uncle asked him as when we can take mom back home??

'By tomorrow she will be perfectly fine and then you can'. He replied and left.

And mom became cynosure of all eyes...

Now, that mom is back home, a nurse looks after her so I can concentrate on my studies since exams are just 5 days away. Zed and I did combine study, we actually had fun.

Finally exam day arrived and mom had herself packed my bag with all necessary thing which I didn't have to cross check again and so I touched her feet and walked out. I was so nervous and overwhelming and so it continued each day before exam. Finally our exams were done and we were free from books, restriction, etc.. All we did was have fun, hang out with friends, playing and watching movies..

Chapter Eight
2 Months later:

* * *

I called him 10 times since morning results! results! results! I cribbed. He was already scared and I scared him even more. Finally, results are out, I got 80% and he got 94%..I was extremely happy for both of us. Anna, Bharat, Raj, Yash, Mehek, Rashi, all scored well. Next day we decided to go for shopping. I made him wait for almost 3 hours alone for my shopping, I picked all strapless, backless, cleavage revealing, off shoulder, shorts, torn jeans, jackets, and he made faces when I picked each one of them and gave imploring looks.

"Now, that I am done let's start your shopping", I said.

"No, I am fine. Get in the car I will drop you home" he said and walked away.

I chased him and stopped. "What happen?"

"You have already wasted three hours alone for your shopping", He said, "And I really hate your choice" he said angrily.

"I did not buy it for you, they are for me", I said and smiled.

"Get in the car", he said.

"Ok ok wait just 30 min more. You wait right here I will be back. I will buy the best for you", I said.

"Oh for God's sake no thanks".

"Trust me" I said and walked.

I came back and said "Why don't you buy something for me and give an example of your choice" and I walked away without waiting for him to respond.

I ran in a nearby shop and chose the best colored shirts, jackets and shoes.

I met him exactly after 30 min and threw all those bags on his face and left him to manage it all on his own.

"Keys", I demanded.

"Gladly" he said and threw towards me.

I drove all the way and parked car right in front of an ophthalmology hospital and I had already taken an appointment for Zed and he was like an alien, absolutely no clue. I dragged him out of car and he had no idea what I was exactly doing.

"Where are we going?"

"SSSHHHuuu !!!"

"OK", he said.

"I am here to meet Dr. Sahani" I said.

"Do you have appointment?", the receptionist asked.

"Yes" I told and took out the appointment form and showed her.

He looked totally puzzled.

"What" I asked?

"I should be asking you that Nishk", he said narrowing his eyes.

"Straight and then first left", the receptionist said and smiled.

Now, we are in front of Dr. Sahani and he examines with Zed's eyes and follows a few procedures and then completes the formalities required for lens and we leave.

"When are we supposed to come back", I asked

the receptionist.

"Tomorrow evening Ma'am", she says and we left. "Crazy, incredible girl you are", he said and pulled the keys from my hand and drove me home.

One fine day mom and I had an argument and I left home and drove to my favorite garden away from my home. Hours passed and mom was worried as I did not receive any of her calls and she knew nothing about my whereabouts.

Mom called Zed immediately and he came to me within few minutes. When our eyes met, I buried my face in his shirt and kept weeping. After sometime I burst out laughing and Zed joined me. In his presence, all my problems seems to be silly. I simply forget them.

I held his hand, rested on his shoulder and closed my eyes. "I want to do my engineering in the US, it's my dream", he said at once.

"Hmmm". I replied.

"Are you ok with it Nishk?",He asked in a low voice.

"I am happy with whatever you chose. You will definitely excel". I replied.

There was silence for some time and then he asked "what you wanna do ??"

I narrow my eyes at him and asked "don't you know till now?"

"No, really tell me what is it?"

"The clothes I picked at the mall..." And he cuts me and said it aloud "lemme guess model or actor".

I blushed.

"Model" I said and he gave a wary smile.

After lots of talking he said

"Let's go home", and we headed towards home.

I went straight to my room, when my mom opened door for us and a while later Zed left.

I took my admission in designing and Zed for MPC (maths, physics, chemistry) for next two years. Before starting our college life, we all friends decided to have a bash and so we got permission to celebrate at Oberoi's farm house on the outskirts. Almost all my friends were invited and added to that Zed's new friends Daniel and Rohit. Daniel is half British and half Punjabi and Rohit is a parsi boy. I am very glad that Zed has new friends and will accompany him for next two years in college.

Zed and I stood in a corner looking and smiling at every one and then Raj approached me asking for dance. I immediately slip my hand into his and within no time we were on the dance floor. Raj and I were dancing, talking and laughing and the music went loud every passing second and we were having fun accordingly. After a while, Zed comes on the dance floor and takes my hand off Raj's and helped me gently. Raj excused himself. We began to dance and suddenly slow music began playing in the background. we moved slowly according to the rhythm, holding each other's hand, his hands over my waist, I held his shoulder and distance as such no air can pass through. I went numb for those couple of minutes. The close proximity between us was something new that I felt. I could no longer look into his eyes and simply smiled. I could feel his breath over my bare neck and shoulder.

His cologne filled my nostril. I never knew his close proximity could have so much effect on me.

It was the first time I felt something for Zed and I was totally unaware of this so-called feeling. And we became partners for the entire evening, participated in paper dance where I felt a bit uncomfortable and to break the awkward silence I asked "What did you buy for me the other day at mall"??

After few seconds he said "Just wait for the right time, it will come to you" he whispered, in a complete seductive voice.

Shiver ran down my spine and I blushed again. I rolled my eyes at the back of my head. I loved it though. We enjoyed the entire evening and by now it was midnight, so we decided to leave. Zed dropped me back home. I gave a quick peek on his cheeks and tried to step out of the car, but he pulled me by my wrist and we were just an inches away. We looked into each other's eyes, so intense, his eyes were unreadable, he held my chin up, lips inches apart and suddenly I felt so nervous that I ran out of the car and without even looking back for once, stepped inside my house. It felt extremely different.

I kept tossing and turning in my bed for few hours and could not resist thinking about Zed the entire night.

Chapter Nine

On one such day I did not return home from college though it was around seven in the evening mom was so worried and immediately called Zed.

"Hello Zed is Nishk with you?"

"No aunty. What happen?"

"She did not return from college yet. And it is seven now. Where would this girl be??", She said in a complete worried tone.

"Aunty don't worry, I will call Anna, Mehek and everyone. You please don't worry".

Zed I called everyone but couldn't get any clue..

"Ok aunty I will get her, you Please don't worry" he assured and went looking for her.

He searched in college, asked the guards and asked in the neighboring shops showing my photo but he couldn't find any information. Tension grew more and more as it had turned dark. My mom kept calling him repeatedly. A beggar saw him and asked "are you searching for that girl", "that girl" she repeated and started jumping and laughing. That beggar was in torn dirty clothes with pale dusty skin and dry hair.

"Do you know this girl?" He asked her showing the picture curiously.

"Yes", she said and started jumping over again. She was mad. She took the photo and tore into pieces and ran away. He was taken aback with what just happened. He walked and then stood beside a mosque and prayed to see her soon. His eyes kept scanning every corner of the place on the road. He finally saw me standing near a small puncture shop. He thanked God and crossed the road in a hurry and finally stood in front of me. I was shocked seeing him. "What the hell you think of yourself? You freaking nuts!" He literally yelled at me. People stared at us. I doubled my voice and asked "how dare you shout at me??" "I was just..." and I cut him by saying shut up..

I paid the puncture charges and walked silently. He came chasing me and apologized. "Hey listen Nishk, I have been worried about you. Aunty called me and said you did not return. So I was just searching for you like a mad man and you are being so rude". He stopped, waiting for my response but I kept walking.

"Nishk please" he insisted, "your silence is goddamn.. Sorry", he repeated .

I was upset that how he can he scold indulgently. I started my scooty and drove all the way home. I reached home and mom asked me so many questions at once and then I calmed her down.

"I left college and then I felt something wrong with my vehicle and guess what! The tire punctured and I had to walk with the scooty and couldn't find any repair shop nearby and then finally I found one and it took much more time than expected". I told the whole story dramatically and I knew what question she would shoot so before she asked, I said "My phone switched off and so I could not tell you", I said.

"ahhh" she said.

I took the phone out of my jeans pocket and kept for charging and then mom said, "You scared the hell out of me and I called Zed, he told he would bring you home".

"Did you meet him??"

"No", I said.

"Oh let me inform him" she said and dialed, he steped at the door.

"There you are", mom said.

"Aunty she is being so rude to me when I asked her, what happened".

Mom gave a shocking look at me. I could read her expression as I lied to her.

Mom understood our situation and she thanked him and told the entire story.

"Nishk" he said and I cut him again by saying "if you are that concerned why don't you become my driver??", I said too rudely.

Mom yelled my name aloud.

"Be ready in the morning. I will come to pick" he said, hugged mom and left me in shock.

That evening mom and I had dinner in silence. As always I woke up late and there I heard him honking, I immediately walked to the window and there he was. I was surprised, I knew he was serious but never knew it would be so quick and since then he dropped and picked me from college. I often made him wait for more than hours. I made many friends at college. I introduced Zed to my gang. I became the cheerleader in my college and scored well in academics. Zed too did well. I made him write my assignments keeping him up whole night and I had parties to attend. He never complained. He was there when I was sick. Meanwhile I was hunting for internship, I was keen on entering in modeling as soon as possible. I would give up studies over modeling but couldn't find any opportunity.

Smoothly everything went on well and every single day we fought, laughed after every fight, hang out together, pranks, friend's birthday party, movies, bitchy talks, gossips were all part of my life. I had fun every time. I loved my life and my mom. A very small and occupied life. Nothing to worry about.

Days kept passing and finally the day had arrived when Zed had to leave for US for higher studies. I had no idea, how rapidly time passed and I was always confused with the feelings I had for him. Neither can I talk about this to mom nor zed. It drove me crazy every time I think about it. He got admission in the top college I was happy for him but something held me back like I didn't want him to go far away from me, though I did not tell him, since his parents were happy. I did not want to ruin it. Anyway, he would come back in five years but five years…....five years I kept reciting it in my mind. Oh God what's happening? I was finding it difficult to say a single word.

All those strange feelings struck my mind as if I was watching a movie, I cared him more than required, when ever I got close to him I took a step back, the most awkward silences. I blush when he cracked jokes, held my hand....

I was disturbed when mom came in and told "Zed is here to see you".

"I'll come" I said and walked out taking every single step slowly as my heart beat increased faster and faster as I closed the distance between us and stood exactly in front of him in the hall looking straight into his eyes. We were just five centimeters away. I could feel his breath. We stared at each other without a word. His eyes were trying to tell me something which even he did not know and I could not read. His expressions were not the usual. I could find him slightly different today. Mom came with a glass of water and I moved away. He took out a cover from behind and handed it over to me and said "I told you when time comes you will get your gift and right now is the right time".

I looked straight into his eyes and then inside the cover was a dress.

It was a white and red mixed floor length frock that I had never worn before.

I thanked him. Which I never did in the past. "Today is my last day in India and I want to be with you for those last moments, with my only best friend. Will you??"

He asked extending his hand out. Tears swam in my eyes and I slipped my hand into his and said "Yes".

I changed immediately and wore a shoulder length earrings, bangles. Mom was stunned and liked my new look and said "I would buy you few more like this. You look damn pretty my baby" she said and kissed my forehead.

He touched mom's feet and hugged her. Mom blessed him and told not to forget her and smiled. She prepared his favorite cookies and gave him. "Never" he said and we walked hand in hand.

"You are looking beautiful" he said. "I know, as always" I said and nudged him. "No wonder" he said and got into the car. He drove to a nearby temple. It was the first time I had been to a temple, he offered prayers and so did I. I simply joined my hands. He never told me that he often visits this temple because I would have made fun of it. But he bought me here because he wanted to confess something.

He remained silent for few seconds.

"I come here only to thank God because I have got the very best friend. You are my only friend I trust you more than myself, share my feelings, and now I am going across the seven seas and am ready to leave all that only if you stop me. Nothing makes me happy than being close to you", he said in a low and unfeigned way, holding my hand.

He continued, "My only fear is what if you forget me...", he stopped with moisture in his eyes..

I didn't want to ruin his mood or cancel his plans, his dream of studying in US.

I took a long breath and laughed out fighting back my tears. I pushed him back and said "you are no way back compared to hindi serials, so much of drama, chill no way I am not gonna forget you but dare you if you forget me and get into any relationship without telling me. And I won't miss you that much, ok! I will be busy with my modelling career, and I doubt if I would be able to find time for all this, ahh???" I said playfully and hugged him.

"Why don't you come with me?? There are many such colleges and your chances will be high. We both can be together and return together", He said.

"Woow nice idea", I said kiddingly.

"I can't leave mom, Zed. I love her so much" and then silence prevailed.

His face showed the disappointment as he hung his head down. I did not want to hinder his thoughts at that moment.

I pulled him closer and hugged him and told him in his ear "you will always remain close to my heart. I will wait for you" and his face lit up with his radiant smile. He hugged me tightly and said, "he is feeling better now".

I didn't want to give him any tips because he knew how to behave, how to talk, he was well civilized already. We spent some time in my favorite garden. We drove to a small beech near by, had dinner at a restaurant and came home late. We were standing at the gate and I told him I will come along with you to the airport.

"No", he said.

"What?? Why? I mean why ?".

"I dont like the feeling of going away from loved ones right in front of their sight. I feel guilt for abandoning them to fulfill my dreams".

"Loved ones??" I questioned.

He tactfully answered, "yes, so I have asked mom and dad not to come along and now you, please don't act stubborn, I don't want to fight before leaving" he said.

"I am coming that's final", I said and walked in . "Nishk! Nishk!" He shouted and then left as I closed the door.

Chapter Ten
At airport - 7:00 Am

* * *

Zed and I were at airport and the announcement was made. So he got up and took his luggage. Immediately fresh tears rolled down his cheeks, he hugged me and muttered in my ear "don't date any random boys, reach home early or at least inform mom, promise me you will take care of yourself and you will never change. As you said, you will wait for me, promise me Nishk", finally I broke down. I frown at him, at a loss what to say, "yes yes" I promise was all I could say and huge lump forms in my throat and I hugged him tightly. He walked away waving, waving, waving and disappeared.

Chapter Eleven
At hospital:

* * *

Zed's Pov:

At around 10:00, we reached the city hospital and asked at the reception.

"Do you know Nishk?" "Sorry" the receptionist said.

We were confused and looked at each other. Then, Rohit stepped ahead and said, "Actually, we are looking for our friend, who was bought here approximately five years ago and now, that we knew nothing about her this is the last option we left with", he said in a pleading tone.

Emphasizing the situation and without asking any question further she asked for the name. "Kanishka Mathur". All three said in unison and smiled.

"Gimme a minute. Sir", she said.

She gasped and said, "Well sir, I have no clue about this but we have a sister Nancy who is working in the hospital from past 15 years but she works second shift, and I am sure she might be of great help, she keeps check on every patient. Her shift is at 11 so you can meet her till then you will have to wait sir", she said and we said ok and left.

We waited and finally met sister Nancy, a 65 year old. She looked very calm and kind. The following year she would retire.

"Kanishka Mathur, I wanna know about her", I blabbered at once.

She gave me a puzzled look, and asked, "Who are you?".

"I am Zed Oberoi. I am here for your help.

You have been working here since so long and so only you can help us. My friend met with an accident exactly five years ago, she was brought here"

Daniel interrupted saying, "It was you with other doctors, I saw that day".

"Ok but tell me the name of the patient", she asked, looking at our worried and concerned faces.

We said unison "Kanishka Mathur" and her face changed color.

She walked towards her cabin and we followed her without a word.

I sat in front of her, waiting for her to speak up. Few dreadful silent moments passed.

"I cannot forget her, a brave women, her mother" she said lost in her thoughts.

We all three looked at each other.

"When she was bought here….." she shudder to think about what happened and that scared me. As her face told everything.

"Please sister", I pleaded.

"The day she was bought here, she was immediately shifted to emergency. I looked at her carefully, completely in a drenched in blood, every flesh of her body was wounded and bleeding.. Excess blood loss. I was assisting Dr. Jayvardhan. He examined her well and after conducting the tests we were waiting for her to gain conscious. Her mom kept asking as what happen and when will she get to see her daughter. I calmed her saying she will be alright. She said in a low voice. Painful voice. We all thought she would gain conscious probably after 6-7 hours. But 24 hours passed away. Doctor along with other staff was hell worried. It was a case of accident and she had severe injures on her head and bruises all over her body. But we were sure that there is no chance of death. The poor girl was going through lot of pain in that state, where she could not even complain to anyone. I felt death was far better rather seeing her that way. Her mom kept praying to God for her well-being. After few hours Dr. Jayvardhan walked to her mother and asked her to come to his cabin. We were all in a state of perpetual motion in this hospital", she said everything in one go.

She continued, "Dr. told that the reports indicated severe head injuries and damage.

She cut him off by saying, "from the past 24 hours you have been saying the same thing, will you clearly tell me for god damn sake", she yelled at him in a sharp tone.

"I understand", Dr. said and took a heavy breath and continued, "Due to severe damage on the brain and after the final analyses of the reports claim that she has probably slipped into coma. She may recover in a week or months or say years". "It was very hard for her Mom to digest all that she heard. She could not believe all that the Dr. said and the Dr. had no words to console her. I stood by her side sympathizing but she demanded for clear explanation".

And then Dr. said, "We thought this was a case of accident and we followed all that which was supposed to do. But when she did not gain conscious even after 24 hours, then this case seemed to be mysterious, then we consulted a specialist from London, Dr. Paul. He came here and reexamined and then this report was generated. It is a case of FCED, known as Fuchs Corneal Endothelial Dystrophy. A rare disease which could damage brain and…" he paused and finally said "and could even take away her vision. This is one in a million case. And according to research, there are only 7 patients who have gone through this and all seven from various parts of globe".

"There is no cure to this and hence research is still going on. One such patient with this disease was just a 7 year old from China. The other was a female from New Jersey, 32 yrs old. It comes in all age, nothing is certain. The probability of survival is 0.001%. Sometimes even science doesn't have answer to all such questions. We believe in both miracle and science. Have faith in God and let's pray for her altogether".

Dr. Jayvardhan was very kind. He did not know how to express his helplessness. I wondered how beautiful she looked even in such a terrible condition. The oxygen mask over her mouth, stitches all over and injections installed into her delicate skin. She was just breathing, nothing more than that, no movement, no talks, no pain, no cry, no smile, no demands, no complaints, nothing".

Tears started to fall on their own, as she narrated the story.

"Few more days passed and then weeks followed by months and it turned into a year. But there was no sign of recovery. But her mom was strong. She did not lose faith. But, by then the girl face turned pale, the glow was no more, dark circles under her eyes and lips turned dry.. I pitied seeing her transform this way.

By then every doctor, nurses, ward boys and other patients everybody knew about her. Her name was in every ones prayer. Sometimes her friends visited her but I have never seen you. Where were you?", She asked.

I selfishly went to make my career and her life swept off here he thought and silly me, ignored the letter she gave me as well. He thought.

"Kanishka and I are childhood friends. That day she came along with me to airport, though I said no. She never listened to me. If she would have then I guess this disaster would have never happened. As soon as I came back I wanted to meet her badly but my parents knew nothing about her and then I met Daniel who was also at the airport".

She simply nodded.

"Then, what happen?? Now where are they?" I asked.

"Even seasons came quick, summer, rainy winter spring all was just like a rotation of cycle but was no improvement in her condition. Her mom told how much she loved rain. And during winter when she was sick how she cared and all".

She continued, "After five years, God finally showed mercy and she opened her eyes, I was right next to her cleaning the room, she was on the ventilator for all those years, when I noticed the changes in the machine. I hurriedly rushed to the doctor and her mom panicked and so did I and the others. We just hoped it wasn't any bad news but to our utmost surprise that girl opened her eyes and we all were dead surprised. We immediately asked her mom to enter in the room. The girl stared at every one and was shocked looking at doctors and nurses, the machines on her bed side. She kept noticing everything. She scanned and found all unfamiliar face and when her eyes met her mom who was crying she uttered mom and they hugged so tightly. Tears were in every one's eye. Other patients came to see her. They all gathered out of her ward. The news spread soon like fire catch woods. Doctors examined her while she tightly held her mom and said "now she was even good to go home. They all exchanged smiles. That day it wasn't like a hospital. It looked like a heaven happy home".

Her mom kissed her all over face sobbing and saying all lovely words. Nishk's head was heavy by then. She felt pain all over her body. She was scared by the sight. Her mom told all these were praying to God for your well being and she then smiled at every one and whispered thank you in a very low voice.

"Her eyes were deep inside, pale face, dry lips, the skin lost its moisture. Doctor decided to discharge the third day and so we staff decided to celebrate. We brought a cake for her, as we entered in her room she was sitting on bed making faces for all those tasteless food. As she saw the cake she was happy and surprised at the same time. In past five years her mom would get cake to hospital, and distribute among all. And, so they wanted her to cut the cake and cheer up. The same day after few test she was discharged and the smiling face and the most happiest women on earth, her mom was unforgettable. And I knew nothing about them after that where did they go and all", She said wiping her tears.

"When did they leave" he asked. "Three months back", she replied.

Silence....

We all looked at each other and every one's eyes were filled with tears. No one even in their dream ever thought any such thing would happen. But fact was right in front of them and they had to accept the ugly reality.

I got up cleared my throat and said "thank you". We thanked again.

She said, "God bless" and we left. We saw the time and it was three in the morning.

It was very hard to digest this information but was very helpful. I was happy that she was fine now but where would they be. As, we came out of the hospital, I asked Daniel to leave as I wanted some time alone and so he agreed. I felt as if the cold breeze was tearing my heart apart in this wee hours. Then, it began to rain heavily. I walked in rain and kept repeating in mind, "I love you Kanishka, I love you, I love you...."

And hence there was the beginning of **part 2**

Chapter Twelve
After hospital :

* * *

"Mom how long has it been?" Nishk asked?

"Ummm...." She stammered.

"Mom", this time a bit louder.

"5 years..."

"What" she said and rolled her eyes. Almost got up from her bed and the TV remote fell down.

Rushing towards her, her mom explained, "Yes, you met with an accident and was hospitalized immediately and then slipped into coma for five long years. It almost killed me every single day during that period. Many things changed in the past and I have so much to tell. Your recklessness kills me and so I was always behind you but still could not save you from all that... that happened" she said and blamed herself for this.

"Mom....", she said and hugged her and apologized.

"You never for once thought how I would be without you? You never cared what I would do without you. I am here only for you. You being the sole reason for my life" she said and hugged her, kissing all over her face.

"But mom, I could hardly remember anything and my head always spins and I don't even find this place familiar. Where are we?"

"Why do you always have to be so stubborn, I'll tell you all once you become perfectly alright sweety" she said peeking on her cheek.

"Now, I am perfectly fine", she said and then her mom finally gave up.

"Ok promise me, you'll listen to me carefully and accept whatever I say".

She faked a promised as always. And her Mom took a long breath and started……

"Nishk , exactly 4 years back on your birthday I was returning from temple and there I met your dad, my husband".

Her eyes wide open and jaw dropped. "Yes he was there. I did not even want to talk to him but he himself was so alone and lost in his life. He himself wanted to get back to us, get back to you. Initially it was such a tough decision for me to accept him, to forgive him but he was always there for me when your health was so bad. He was the one who made me believe that you will be alright. I almost gave up on you", She said and cried her heart out.

"I forgave him and now I want you too forgive him. He loves you, dear. I have seen the love and worries for you. We are in your father's house. This house is ours, it's yours. To bear hospital's expenses I had to sell our old house, I had no choice left. And now see we look like a perfect family", she said and faked a smile with tears in her eyes.

After a long pause….

"Nishk say something"… she requested and cried.

I turned my face away and tears filled in her eyes. "Mom, when I asked you about dad you never told me a word and so as I grew older I stopped asking you. Now all of a sudden, after so many years out of nowhere dad appears and you expect me to get along and accept the way it is. I can't. I simply can't". She said without looking at her mom and walked out of the room.

As the room ended there was a staircase which led to the hall. As she took a step ahead, she slipped and rolled on the stairs andwent unconscious again.

"Nishk, how are you feeling", her dad asked, taking steps towards her, she ignored and rushed to her mom.

"Talk to your dad".

I looked at him, my dad Mr. Ashok Mathur, middle aged, roughly in 40's tall and handsome, brown eyes with thin black hair and tanned skin dressed in tee and jeans.

I had no clue about his nature. I thought with puzzled face and then looked away without saying a word.

"I am fine but I am bored being in my room. I want to go out and do you know any of my friends because I don't even remember any one".

Her mom was shocked but not scared because the doctors had already told her about such a situation and she was prepared for all that came her way.

"I have not even seen my face and I don't find any mirror in this house".

"I will get a new one in your room" Mom said caressing my hair. And asked her to go to the room. Came to her room. Many questions were running in her mind but her head would ache at the same time.

She heard a knock at the door and saw her dad entering with ice cream in his hand.

"Here is your favourite ice-cream", he said and

she ignored and looked the other way.

"Nishk I ..", he started and she cut him off, "I want to be alone".

There was a sudden disappointment on his face. He turned away to leave and just then she said.

"Thank you for being with mom in those hard times, else she would have been shattered but all I want to say is don't expect anything from me. I can never forgive you for all that pain you gave to me and to my mom. You have no idea what mom had gone through but she raised me so well. Do you even realize the pain of a single parent?".

I questioned dad, looking straight in his eyes with an apologetic face, then mom entered. The room was filled with silence echoing her voice.

"Anyway I am fine now and we don't need you anymore", I said giving a death glare.

The hatred within her, towards her dad had reached such a level that nothing could even fall in place, for her well being he decided to move out.

The decision was tough though. Before leaving he said to his wife, "I am so happy that our daughter is just like her mom, stubborn and beautiful. Trust me, things will be all good", he said wiping her tears, kissed her forehead and left without even looking back once. Her mom loved her dad and that was all she knew later.

Her mom and she spent quality time talking about many things, watching movies, studying. Kanishka was getting better every single day. Every day a little bit.

Chapter Thirteen
3 months later

* * *

Zed's hunt for Nishk had finally paid off when he met her mother in a super market. He saw a lady struggling with her carry bags in both hands,he moved forward to help that's when he saw her face and was dead shocked. She did not recognize him, that's obvious as he changed a lot.

She said thank you and was about to turn then he called her, "Aunty, didn't you recognize me?".

She was puzzled and was thinking, he somehow managed to utter, "Zed!!!", and her face lit up, eyes filled with joy and she took him in an embrace.

She was happy to see him after years.

"You look so handsome", she said cupping his face in her palm, kissing his forehead. He blushed. They walked out and started their conversation.

"How are you aunty and how's Nishk. I heard about Nishk, tried to find you all ever since I have returned but see it took so long" he said disappointedly. He kept asking a number of questions and Mrs. Mathur was tight lipped.

"Let's go home. You'll get all your answers", she said. They entered an apartment which was well decorated and furnished.

"Kanishka!!" her mom shouted and his heart started beating a million times in a second. He did not know how he would react seeing her after so long.

"Yes mom", came the voice from the bedroom.

"Come out look who's here?"

Her voice echoed in his mind and he imagined

that nine years old cute little face of hers in his mind and heart.

"I am sleeping" she said.

"Come out dear, it's a surprise".

"Wooow", she said and jumped out came running and stood right in front of her mom. She looked at her empty hands and asked where the gift was.

"Look", she said and turned to face Zed.

She turned around to see the most handsome guy she had ever seen, 6'1" tall, broad shoulder, dressed in jeans and a tee, thick black shiny hair and lips so luscious and when she looked at his eyes, he was already starring at her. She felt so embarrassed as was caught staring at him and was confused, but a smile crept on her lips. She felt good.

He felt like hugging her tightly. Feeling her close to his heart. Kissing all over her face.

When they looked again at each other, he took a step ahead. "Who is he" she asked and moved a step back waiting for her mom to answer.

His heart broke into millions pieces, it came as a blow in his stomach when he heard those painful words. He feared this would come out of her mouth when they would meet and so it happened.

"Don't you recognize him?" Her mom asked. She shook her head "No", and started walking back to her room.

"He is Zed, your childhood friend". She stood still and turned around in shock, looks like the bell rang and her jaw dropped down. She came forward taking slow steps and pinched his arm.

"Aah", he shouted as it was bit hard.

"Omg, how and when did you turn so handsome. I do remember you but it's just I am sorry...", She kept blabbering in one go and the old Kanishka Mathur was finally back. She dragged him to her room and was shocked to see her room so neat and clean for the first time.

When he looked at her face closely she looked beautiful as always but the bruises on her forehead and arm were clearly noticeably.

Next to her bed was a table where numerous medicines were kept. When he looked at her she was just smiling at nothing. Their eyes spoke hundred words.

The silence, unspoken words between them was something quite unexplainable. But they found comfort in each other. He would stare at her and then look other side when she would catch his sight. Her memories of Zed were quite fresh. She remembered every bit of him.

He tried to converse and began asking series of questions to which she simply smiled without answering even one. Finally he gave up, as she never answered his question way back in those days either.

But he was so happy seeing her. That meant a lot to him. "C'mon tell about yourself" "As you know, I did nothing in the past" she joked and he felt bad for it.

But she was cool about it like nothing had ever happened.

They talked the entire day recollecting their childhood memories, how they first met and burst out laughing, talked about silly incidents, school, college, friends, gossip, party, shopping, later he showed her, his designs of car on her laptop, his friends Jake and everyone, his achievements.

She was so happy. He showed her all his photos, she carefully took glance of each one and then questioned "No girlfriend?". He blushed and said, "No" and immediately switched to another topic, as he knew where it would end up.

"Hey that tattoo, is it still on your lower back", he.

She got up from the bed and raised her top up and showed him.

He felt so embarrassed and asked her to cover herself up and sit. He showed many party pictures and she was super excited seeing that herself being party freak.

She always wanted to get high, dance and all. She is an amazing dancer although. Her mom served snacks and was so happy to see them together. Later they went for a walk, then to their favorite garden.

She was so happy. She just wanted to savor the moment. As she held his hand, shiver ran down his spine.

How much he carved for her touch.

They sat on the bench looking everywhere, talking and time simply passed by. He wanted to spend quality of time with her. He left no chance to let go off her now. They returned home and while having dinner, "how are your parents" Mrs.Mathur asked.

"They are good aunty but why didn't you tell them about Nishk, you thought they were not worth of knowing?",

He questioned and she immediately replied, "No my son, I was all lost and it didn't strike me. Not a single day passed without praying for her, I forgot everyone. Everyone", she whispered.

There was a silence. And they completed rest of the dinner in silence.

"Convey my greetings to your parents", she said and hugged him. She left giving them some private time.

He half hugged Nishk, kissed her forehead and promised to see her tomorrow and left her place.

After reaching home, he narrated the whole story to his parents. They were shocked to hear and were happy as well.

"Did you confess your love?" His mom asked out of curiosity.

"For now, let's just keep it a little secret", he told and decided to see her tomorrow.

As he lay down on bed wearing a smile, soon fell asleep and was excited to meet her again.Next day she quickly woke up early morning, got dressed and eagerly waited for him. But he was late thinking she would be still asleep. Hours later, the Oberio family came and moms looked at each other in a shock and exchanged greetings. Tears of joy rolled down their cheeks. Aunt took Nishk in her embrace and placed a kiss on her forehead. With the bruises on her face, she wasn't looking that beautiful though. They were happy to see her in all good condition. The women carried on their talks while Zed and Nishk went to their room.

Now there is not much of talking between them but just smiling, blushing and stealing glances. And by the end of the day they had dinner and left.

And so Zed kept visiting her every day, surprising her with flowers, chocolates and many gifts, they would often spend time out for movies, in the parks and everywhere.

Both were happy having each other around. They would walk around; sometimes he would take her for shopping, ice creams and always had fun. She would never keep quiet except in sleep. She would speak about anything and everything. Her voice was just music to his ear. Once you love the person whole heartedly, you start accepting and loving everything about them completely ignoring their flaws. Sorrow was long gone. As days passed her bruises and health was getting much better.

And Zed's mom would often ask him to confess his feelings before it was too late. He never payed attention to her words and was just cherishing those moments with her. They would spend hours watching soccer, though she was never interested, she would simply sit beside him. He explained her about the game but it never fascinated her. She would fall asleep soon in the middle of the game burying her face deeper in his chest and sleeping soundlessly. His heart would skip beat. Their close proximity at times would take his breath away.

Things were getting better but the moisture eyes of her mother during nights couldn't be ignored. This made Nishk restless and guilty. She blamed herself for all this.

It had been three hours sitting in front of her laptop and balls of paper scattered all over the floor. She was confused as to write a letter to her dad or preferred to write an email. Finally she started,

To,

My dear dad……

She paused and then immediately erased it. She shut it down and jumped onto bed and drifted to sleep.

At 3:00 Am, again she opened her laptop and began to type…

The fingers made their own way on the keyboard and the magic of the breeze through the window made the room cold.

Chapter Fourteen

* * *

To

Mr. Ashok Mathur,

Well I don't know as what to address you since you and I very well know the reality. And the fact is that you never gave me the honor of calling out to you. Like other girls who call their father as 'dad', or 'papa', or 'daddy' whatever...but fortunately or unfortunately you are my dad and husband of my beloved mom.

I don't know how you are, or say how you were and the thing is that I never want to know either. But the fact which can't be ignored is that mom loves you. She misses you. She was happy when you were around.

And perhaps, I don't want to be the reason for yours separation again. I want you back in her life again. I guess I have never done anything for her so far, but with your help we can give a perfect meaning to her life. I do not wish to hear anything about past, hence let's just forget and move ahead.

There are many complaints more than my age, don't know where do I even begin from. I don't even remember you holding my small hands in your hand and walking or carrying me in your arms, how much I ever missed it. I wish you were there when I was in a school, attending every event and clapping for me when I did stage performances. I always asked mom to keep a vacant chair besides her hoping you would appear any time soon. But that never happened. I wish you were there when I enrolled myself in college. I wish you would scolded me for getting a tattoo on my lower back like any father would. I wish you would advise me to stop

chasing boys like any father of a teenager would worry. I wish you were beside mom when she was ill, making her feel easy, I wish you were there when we were financially weak, untill granny helped us. I wish you would come searching for me when I was gone away from home for a long times. I wish you would restrict me from many things. I wish you would teach me few things that could be just special for both of us. I wish you would have slapped me for smoking, I wished to run to you when I was upset with mom. I wished and wished and wished and wished...

But time has moved on and so did I. Now there is one final thing left for which I really need your help. Mom!!. I want you two to get back on really good terms once and forever. And then that would be happy ending like my Disney princess stories.

If you wish to join hands, do reply else you can simply ignore. Whatever is your reply make sure it's just between us. "SECRET"

Bye
Kanishka mathur...

After typing, she froze for seconds before hitting enter. She smiled at the screen and said "good night" and went back to sleep.

Next morning, when she opened her eyes everything seemed so blur. She was not able to see things clearly which were near to her. She rushed to the washroom and splashed water multiple times over her face and eyes and then everything was alright. Later she got carried with her work.

It's been three days she had sent an email.

Excitedly she opened her laptop, and there was a message waiting for her and she hurriedly clicked on it. It read...

To,

My dear princess,

I know I am responsible for all that problems caused to you and your beloved mother and I apologize for that whole heartedly. I am very glad you gave me another chance and I promise to not disappoint you. I regret for not being at all those moments. Believe me or not I missed both of you and never had a peaceful sleep throughout my life. It was not that I never wished to get back to you but I was ashamed for all that I did and made life miserable for everyone. I was not even present for my own dad's funeral. I have many regrets.

You sow a seed in both of our lives now. And so I have a perfect reason to live. I am proud of you as well. Call me whatever your heart says.

Love you,

Your dad.

She smiled but did not understand how to react to it. A lot of questions revolved in her mind but had no clue how to resolve. She was happy to read "princess" and went back to bed.

On a fine day, she insisted her mom that she would go herself and buy brown bread and so her mom agreed. She took her parcel and was returning home. Suddenly while crossing the road, her eyes went blur again. She could not see the moving vehicles and was terrified. She rubbed her eyes but still no use. Out of nowhere, Zed reach her and patted on her shoulder completely surprising her. She recognized his voice. She asked him to buy water and then splashed water on her face and emptied the bottle. She felt better.

She felt utterly happy seeing him.

He teasingly asked her, "What was wrong??" And she nudged him and said, "Nothing", they started walking towards home.

Throughout the drive, he kept her entertained, talking about lot more stuff. He never wanted the smile on her lips to fade away. He purposely complimented her but she wasn't someone who would fall for compliments and gifts.. Later she told him about the email. He was shocked but was happy that things started moving smoothly in her life.

She started, "Life is too short. You never know when, what, where or how it all happens. We make mistakes, we learn from mistakes. Every person has the right to make mistakes. Everyone deserves a second chance. We have limited people in our lives........., so just love them.........., forgive them......... and be happy always........ Cherish every moment.........." taking deep pauses after each word.

He cut her midway and could not understand as what she was blabbering. What made her say all those but it all made sense. Even she was confused. He kissed her cheeks, dropped her at her place and left.

Chapter Fifteen

While browsing through the Internet she saw the auditions for Miss Femina. She immediately read the requirement and incidentally she was eligible, impatiently filled the form accepting the terms and condition. She was overjoyed, this was the much awaited moment in her life. She registered and ran to her mom downstairs.

Her mom was happy hearing this and they both came back to her room. She stood in front of her full length mirror, keenly looked at her self. On clearly observing, she found rough silky long hair, tanned arms, unmoistured skin, well curved figure, the painful eyes filled with sorrow, the lines on her temple, and the redness on her cheeks....

A lot has to be done but how she screamed and looked at her mom for help.

She suggested first to calm down and wait for the shortlisted candidate list that would be announced within the next 24 hours. She huffed with sarcasm.

She called Zed and told him about the registration.

She was worried if they would shortlist her or not?

Would they like her pictures?

Later she realized that she has registered at the last moment since, it was the last day.

Would they consider?

He gave positive hopes and boosted her with confidence and now both were eagerly waiting for the results.

She opened her laptop for about 15 times checking her inbox and then there was a mail from her dad. She ignored at once but to kill time she clicked on it...

To,

My dear princess,

How are you? Have not received any response from you so I decided to write. How are you doing my lil princess? Miss you....

I keep reading your previous mail often, every time I read, it sounds so fresh. In past my email would be flooded with loads of my work. I was never so desperate to check my email every 10 minutes.

Lots of love,

Papa.

On reading this, she felt so better. She believed her family would be complete soon and definitely one fine day all three would be under same roof. She wanted to reply but shut her laptop and lay down on the bed.

Soon, she was fast asleep, the room filled with her innocent thought which no one could ever hear. At such an early age she had faced so much. As they say good follows bad and bad follows good.... The cycle goes on and on..

She woke up hours later and immediately opened her laptop. She found a new mail from miss Femina team. She eagerly clicked and read till end and was happy that she got through. She rushed to her mom, hugged her tightly. Her mom understood everything and she informed participants are supposed to move to Mumbai for further rounds. She informed Zed with all enthusiasm and within no time to surprise her, Zed called upon all her friends, Daniel, Rohit, Anna, Mehak and Rashi. In growing up years though they were not much of a part but for good old time, the importance never fade away. The friends with whom we laughed, we cried are someone we should never forget in life.

Everybody was happy for her. They all decided to go for shopping to buy all the necessary stuff and later the girls headed for salon. It looked like clock had made fast motion. The journey to Mumbai was well planned. Zed, Kani along with her mom were all set for their Mumbai trip. They boarded the flight, rooms were already booked for the participants, so Zed and Mrs. Mathur were staying at hotel. It was all a happy go lucky moment. She was so nervous to step into the auditorium. She looked at her mom one last time, they exchanged smile and stepped in. On entering, she was greeted by a beautiful women dressed in short black dress and curly hair, colored at the bottom and a batch was given, which was supposed to be attach to her dress. Further she looked around and found all girls beautifully dressed and makeup caked on their faces, they were tall, slim, perfect curves, wearing 6-7 inches stiletto heels and killer eyes that would seduce any man in seconds and her nervousness knew no bound. There, on the podium was a good looking man, holding a mike and announced, "Attention please, all beautiful young ladies. Well, thank you", he said with a bright smile as everyone looked at him.

"First of all, heartiest congratulation to all the participants. Out of 9,000 registrations we have filtered top 100 and here you all are. So, big round of applause for yourself". And the crowd went gaga and cheered loud along started hooting. That was very proud moment for her as well but she was not so comfortable among strangers. All she wanted to do was go back to her mom. Well we have organized a party at the beach side in the evening, a welcome party so see you all around", the host said, who introduced himself as Vishal having a dragon size tattoos on his biceps.

Girls around were in a group, laughing, giggling and few might obviously be bitching. One such female was making weird eye contacts with Vishal and he was completely enjoying it, responded back in lustful eyes.

Nishk turned around and found her way to the room, took shower and called mom and told everything, her mom advised to be careful and advised not to drink. Later she hung up the phone and lay on bed. Soon a thought hit her mind and she opened her laptop, did not find any new message from her dad so herself immediately started typing....

Dear papa,

I have got something really important to tell you. Mom and I are in Mumbai. I have been shortlisted for Femina Miss India. You did not know, but I wanted to be a top model.

I was very nervous papa, I was actually scared

today. I was losing my confidence. I don't want to let down mom. I feel so low. I could not share all these with her because she gets stressed easily and I don't want to trouble her. I miss you papa...

There she left the incomplete message and hit the send button. She closed her laptop and had a peaceful four hour long sleep.

She attended the party and was soon bored faking smiles at random people. Everyone were in group, holding a glass of wine for fashion. She hardly knew anybody and within no time she was back to her room, texted her mom and drifted to sleep.

The next morning everyone had assembled at pool side. The first round, symmetry round would start in two hours, they were instructed to get prepared as it was an mass elimination round. It was very clearly mentioned that out of the hundred present there, only twenty would proceed to the further rounds. Further, ten participants would directly move to the finale week which was just three weeks away. Further information would be revealed to the participants only who would make to the next round.

She got back to the room and opened her wardrobe, which had all glamorous cloths. She picked a bikini suit, which was conservatively presentable. Soon, the event started where everyone was dressed in their best and tension could be clearly seen on their faces but they were masked with fake smiles. Few made disgusting faces seeing one another and race to be in top 20 was very challenging.

Tension grew more within her but did not know

how she was going to manage. Soon one by one they went in and she was the 57th participant. When they announced participant no 57, she made her move. As she entered, she keenly observed the stage which was in a perfect long L-shap and seven judges sitting straight, pair of seven eyes directly staring at her. Shiver ran down her spine but she built the confidence within herself and began to walk, carrying pride, her beautiful face shining in those dim lights, her two piece which was conservatively presentable and perfect according to the theme, six inches heel, exposing her hour glass figure and well-toned skin , wearing a smile throughout the one minute walk, flawlessly exposing her tattoo on her lower back which was very sexy. She was well aware that the judgment would be focused on the beauty of face, figure, and physical fitness and most importantly the confidence they carry. She wore a natural smile throughout and one last before leaving. She saw the judges scribbling something and whispering to each other but did not let her focus shift, just went with the flow.

As soon as she came out she let out a deep breath which she was holding and was not aware of. She quickly changed her dress and was eagerly waiting for the round to complete, and results to be announced. She waited for hours in the waiting hall along with other participants and interacted with a few girls who were actually good and from different corners of the map. Many of their parents did not even support but they made their way towards their dream. She felt happy that her parents supported her, being there for her, protecting her. She did not want any bonding but was glad she found few kind people around. After the much awaited time, they all were asked to assemble at the auditorium, the same place where they assembled on the very first day. She closed her eyes while vishal was announcing the names. The last and final, who made in top 20 is he said took a long pause looking the crowd where many girls let out tears and she crossed her finger hoping her name to be heard and to her utmost surprise he announced "Kanishka Mathur, participant no.57". A big smile was plastered on her lips, overwhelmed, ultimately the eliminated participants were supposed to leave the venue immediately. As she turned to leave, a girl came from behind who had a piercing on her eyebrow, with whom she was sitting in the waiting hall, hugged her tightly and congratulated.

"Both of us are in!" she said and laughed. It clearly resembled her excitement.

She looked at her smiling face and gave a nod. "Hi I am Zara", she said and extended her hand. "Hi", she introduced herself on their way back to rooms. She immediately called her mom and told everything, so fast that she was on cloud nine.

"I miss you. I want to meet you guys now", she said.. Zed was also happy and wished to see her immediately. He already missed her for those days.

After talking for about 45 min she hung up the call and opened her laptop to see had received any mail from her dad.

Dear princess,

I am glad to hear this news and also happy that you are close to your dream.. I am proud of you. You can never let anyone down. Believe in yourself and everything will fall in place, just don't worry. I am sure even your mom must be proud of you. Eagerly, waiting for your reply.

Lots of love
Papa.

She was happy reading this and immediately wrote a reply describing everything right from her nervousness, those girls, Zara, judges, the place and how eighty people were simply eliminated. She typed such a long text and laughed sheepishly. And hit the send button. That day in the evening she heard a knock on her door and went to open it. As the door flung open, Zara hugged her and jumped on her bed looking everywhere. They sat and kept talking, she felt as if she was invading her personal space but it's just that she was trying to be friendly. She told she got cosmetic surgery done for this competition and her eyes went wide open and dropped down her jaw. They talked for some time, had dinner and later they debated on how the judgment would be done, the criteria, she told her about her mom and Zed, and that's when her smile disappeared because Zara lost her mom when she was 5. later talked for some time and both dozed off.

Next day everyone gathered at the same place for the second round to begin and this time another ten would be eliminated. This round was a group comparison and all had to wear their best dress. At this round, they were supposed to display their body in the most glamorous and graceful way. Any length of the dress would be accepted. She picked her clothes, a strapless floor length dress, which had a cut at the right side of her dress, right from her thighs to the bottom, exposing her well-shaped thighs. Red colored dark lipstick, her naturally straight hair were curled at the end in a wavy fashion. Blush on her cheeks and mascara suitably applied in a decent way. Finally a 6.2 inches classy stilettos heel and she was perfectly ready. She saw Zara coming her way, who was looking fabulous in her pink dress just like Barbie and then the host announced her name on the stage, she winked at Nishk and walked the ramp. She felt how perfect she was from the sight of the back stage. She wondered how she could do that as the other day she was cursing one of the judge being a biggest jerk. And then made her way out of the stage. I hugged her and smiled. As Kanishka was the last participant she was so worried and Zara constantly calmed her by using her sweet words. And finally all 19 were done, her name was announced and when she took a step ahead she missed it, immediately Zara came by her side. She held her tightly, she could not see anything. Her eyes went blur again, felt like being paralyzed below knee. She repeatedly rubbed her eyes multiple times, asked for water and immediately Zara bought it, she sprinkled few drops of water on her eyes and rubbed them again and then felt better. Well by then her makeup over her eyes was completely ruined. Zara cleaned and applied mascara beautifully by then her name was announced twice and finally when she heard Vishal calling her name one last time, Zara pushed her on the stage. Else she would have been disqualified.

Chapter Sixteen

* * *

Kanishka's POV

I looked in shock where 7 pair of eyes were waiting for me. I walked the ramp plastering a nervous yet confident smile, flawlessly making my way on the big 8-shaped stage. As I took every step closer covering the sides of "8" looking at every judge's eye and smiling consistently, moving my body in first left, showing off the perfect curve where the dress perfectly hugged my skin, and then right, the photographers on either ends of the stage constantly clicked pictures which made me smile even more brightly, because this is what I always wanted, right from childhood. I posed confidently standing at the intersection of the 8, and made my way out of the ramp. There I saw Zara worried and immediately took me aside, checked my eyes as if she was a doctor. I said it was fine and assured her with a smile. And then later it was announced that Zara and I were in the top 10 now.

A big party was arranged that night, where few celebrities also came, and that was the first time we interacted with the judges. Well I did not know much about anyone and if Zara was not by my side I would have been so bored.

Zara and I had become very close friends. I dearly adored her. One of the judge named Nishanth Singhania, one of the leading Indian business tycoon and fashionista came on the podium, addressed us with his speech and flirtatious dialogue for which Zara kept commenting. Zara knew everything about them. She told he had married thrice and now currently he's still single, some problems in his married life.

"Such a jinxed creature", she said and I nudged her playfully.

Well the competition got tougher, and we looked at each other, just the lucky one was going to be the Miss feminine India who would be representing India at Lakme fashion week, in Paris. My jaw dropped down when I heard this and Zara too looked surprised, so were the other participants. No one knew about this but smiles were on every one's face. And cash prize of 50 lakhs, a villa, and a car which would be launched within couple of days would be gifted to the winner. The participants clapped aloud.

"This week is gonna be the toughest as well challenging", as I said "so be prepared".

"All the best", he said and passed the mike to Shefali, another judge.

"Bitch!!", Zara muttered under her breath but I heard it. I gave a dead look at her and then back to stage.

"Congratulations to one and all. So we have set a perfect straight forward guideline and breaching any of the rule or any action noticed will not be tolerated which will directly leads to disqualification. So better be careful. Fully focus on yourself, don't plot anything against your fellow participants. As already told, any such incidents noticed will lead to direct disqualification", she said stressing on the last word particularly.

"So now let's see the score board, perhaps the judging criteria, right from your first round and everyone looked at the projector. At the top, Kanishka

Mathur was displayed and I was in awe. My smile brightened and face turned tomato shades. Few girls just glared at me, I ignored everyone, Zara gave me a friendly hug and was actually happy. Zara was never jealous like other girls, she never even cared for my score or anything, I wonder why is she still here.

Every one congratulated me and how badly I wanted to tell mom, dad and Zed, it had been many days I couldn't even talk to them properly. Later it was announced that we have to show our mettle, our talent, beauty with brain.

"So you have one week, be prepared for your big day", she said.

I tasted vodka for the first time at the party, both Zara and I danced like crazy on hit songs, had dinner and left. Next day after seeking permission from Vishal I went to meet Zed and mom.

Zara came along. I hugged my mom as soon as I saw her, then half hugged Zed. I introduced Zara to mom and Zed. Zed greeted Zara and mom half hugged her. Zara was in shorts and a crop top along with a netted jacket. Mom looked her keenly, and then her piercing, "just like a sister", mom said and everyone laughed.

I kept telling about so many things. I told about Paris, cash prize, car and I was super excited. Then mom smiled and asked Zara to tell about herself.

She smiled and said, "Well I lost my mom at the age of five but looking at your love, the gap in my heart just filled with joy. I live with my dad in Singapore, I am a doctor, ophthalmologist, and I am on leave for a month just to participate this".

We all looked in shock at her. "What the fuck, you are doctor I blurred out aloud!!"

She winked at me and left us all shocked.

"I just wanted to experience this too. Dad told me that mom wanted me to become a doctor but then I wanted to become a model, dad supported both and so I am here", she said.

We all loved her. "There was no sign of her being a doctor. She doesn't look like doctor in any angle.", I said and we all laughed. We ordered food, ate happily and went back to our room.

The schedule was perfectly planned by the jury. We all had personal photographers around us. Almost everyone knew Zara and me. We talked to our fellow competitors, and we were taken to different locations for the photo shoot in a best way possible; beaches, forest, hills, and dungeons too. Since Zara loved photography too, she would click my random pictures every now and then, she would say I have killer looks.

"So what are you going to perform as your last performance", I asked.

"Singing yayyy", she said and I was surprised.

"Such a multi talented girl you are" I said and winked at her.

"What about you?", she asked

"Sword dance with ballet touch" I said with a proud smiled.

"Wooow interesting. I would love to see the dance".

"I would love to hear you sing".

We both laughed in unison.

"Who was that guy with your mom?", she asked. "Your boyfriend?" She asked which sounded rather an answer itself.

"No..noo...",I started stammering and she asked to spill the beans in one go in a sharp tone.

I gave up and said "it's complicated, I donno. I mean I seriously donno. We are childhood friends. Later he went abroad for higher studies and I slipped into coma for 5 years and then out of nowhere, he comes and lights up my world and I don't know if he does love me or not because he has never confessed". I said without even looking at her.

"Leave about him. Do you love him?", she asked again in a sharp tone.

"I donno", I said.

She ran fingers through her hairs in frustration.

"Five years in coma, like seriously", she asked as if I was kidding.

I simply nod.

"Well what was the reason?"

"A fatal accident", I said casually.

For the week I strictly followed my diet and at times when my eyes went blur all of sudden I would panic and later everything would be good. I thought it was due to stress or lack of sleep.

Zara would practice singing and I would be mesmerize. How beautifully she sang. She was a tough competitor though.

Eventually when I told mom about sword dance performance she freaked out but later held enough confidence in herself and boosted me.

Zed was also scared but had no choice. I would not listen to anyone. I practiced for hours together. Zara would help me in performing lifts and arranging the swords. Without her support things wouldn't have been so smooth.

Chapter Seventeen

I opened my laptop, wrote a mail.......

Dear papa,

Sorry dad. It's been very tiresome days and so yea things have changed to better but much awaited challenge is fortnight. I want you to come here on my finale day, standing right beside mom, both cheering for me together. I would be happy to see you. This would be a surprise for mom and a small gift from my end. Finally, time for a union forever.

Hope to see you.

Lots of love.

Next day during rehearsal, while performing a jump, I missed a rhythm due to my cloudy vision and fell on the floor just an inch away from the swords arranged around. Zara came to my rescue and looked at my eyes, well I was not able to look at her. She immediately brought water and splashed over my face. I rubbed my eyes and wiped the water of my face. As she was visible to my eye I saw a worried expression on her face. She looked scared.

I said, "I am fine" and assured her and then she reminded me that she is a doctor in a sharp tone.

"Look stop all this, I need to do some tests, if everything is good go ahead and perform, else I am not going to let you do this stupidity", she said.

"How can you say so when we are just a day away from our competition? I told you, I am fine", I said in a rude tone. My sudden behavior hurt her bad and she left me alone. "She was not serious about this competition but I was", I said to myself and resumed my rehearsal.

In evening I went to Zara's room and knocked but it was half open. I saw her, she gestured to come in and closed the door from behind.

"Hey I am sorry, I was rude", I apologized. "Hey relax chill. It's perfectly cool", she said and we exchanged a hug.

"I am worried it's something very bad", she said. "After the competition I am gonna be your patient I promise", I joked and we both laughed.

"I am going to see my mom, would you like to come?", I asked and she immediately agreed.

"Aunt there is something wrong with her eyes, she doesn't say anything but I suspect it's something serious", she said looking at me.

I gave a death glare at Zara.

My mom looked at me for an explanation and then I said, "Due to stress or lack of sleep may be just headache, and a blurry vision".

"I am just worried that I don't get blurred on stage", I said sarcastically.

Mom looked worried and to make her feel better Zed joked, "Well what's the shape of your stage,

Zara said, "Perfect 8-shape, raised her hands and designed in air. "Well in that case take perfect 10 long steps crisscross and the 5 mid point, just pose left right left right and walk back simple" and we all burst out laughing.

I threw a pillow at him for making fun of me.

I saw Zara and mom talking about something in the kitchen while I was with Zed.

"After this competition make me a promise that you gonna donate your time to me my, diva friend!", Zed said teasingly.

I slapped him and as we moved closer to each other, the close proximity between us made me blush and then Zara and mom came and so we moved away.

"Let's leave", I said and "there is a surprise for you, Mom tomorrow" I said and waved bye.

Next day all the girls were busy in their own world. This was the day everyone waited for. All of them were perfectly dressed. I was too nervous. I wore the perfect mid thigh black frock whose bottom below was made of feather, and a pearl necklace with diamond studded for the performance. I was confident about my performance but was not sure would it reach upto their expectations since I heard from Zara that other participants are also performing various dance forms.

For our formal introduction we were supposed to walk the ramp with other male model who would be sharing the same stage. It was well planned in advance and we'd already been told about our partners or might have even mentioned on the contract which I haven't read before signing. My partner was Reyansh, a well-known model, he was friendly. We both walked as he slid his hand around my waist and we smiled at every one and stood at our position along with other nine pairs. I saw my mom and Zed in the crowd who were sitting in the front row clapping for me. I was so proud and so were they. The photographers all around were constantly clicking, taking pictures. Top magazine directors had also assembled to sign a contract with the models and what not. Many celebrities and brand ambassadors were present there but my eyes were searching for only one person whom I wanted right now so badly, my dad. Vishal welcomed us and the crowd applauded so loud and brought me back from my thoughts. We all went backstage leaving the stage in a professional way. As I reached backstage, I saw a women looking out for me, as our eyes met she came to me and said "Someone is here to see you" and I knew who it was. I saw him standing there in black blazer with a bouquet, as our eyes met I ran to him and hugged him tightly, he planted a kiss on my forehead and handed the bouquet and called me princess. "You look damn beautiful my Barbie doll", he said.

I blushed like a teenager. I went to Zara and dialed mom's no. And asked her to come back stage in hurry tone and within no time she reached along with Zed.

When she saw dad, her face changed colour and blank expression which was asking hell lot of questions. Zed was just looking at me, as he had never seen my dad so he had no clue.

I held dad's hand and took mom's hand and bought them close. Tears rolled down her cheeks. I handed the bouquet to him signaling him to give to her and he did as I said. We hugged each other and then Vishal interrupted and asked to get ready, next would be me performing.

I said bye and rushed to change and asked them to see my performance, all the while Zara was looking at me with dumbstruck face. I immediately changed my dress and was on stage as my name was announced.

Chapter Eighteen

The stage was perfectly arranged according to my act. Swords all over and an Arabic song which I had chosen, before starting the act I kissed the floor, looked at my parents, Zed and they smiled. The crowd cheered when I looked at the judges, they were all eager to see my act, I gave a natural quick smile. As the song played in the background I started with the rhythm and my body was making its move magically according to the flow. The foundation, the flawless curvature of my finger and picking the sword skillfully from either sides, the audience looked fascinated as what would be my next move, and performing the stunts beautifully setting a perfect example of dance, without missing a beat, playing with props was always been fun for me, then balanced the sword placing on my head which was resting on my headdress, thankfully it was balanced, then I placed the sword on my hip and went with the flow, making every move aesthetically, finally I stood on my toe and spun like a fairy and slowed down like an angel along the music, my feet lifted inches above the ground and finally I bowed down before leaving and that's when I could see the judges giving an standing ovation, the crowd cheering once more. I was completely dwelled in the dance, this act of mine was like a dream come true. 'A Sword dance'. I looked at my parents, tears of joy flowed down. I bowed down once again and made my way back stage, Zara hugged me so tightly. "Awesome, fabulous" she said and hugged again. I jumped in happiness, next, Zara was immediately called on stage. She sang a song in her beautiful voice and soon joined me back stage. Other girls too performed well, hip hop, belly dance, and many more awestruck dance forms. I did not know if I lose this competition how would I feel because I had gained everything on this platform. My parents were the happiest couple on this planet. Zed also was here. I met Zara. It was all just perfect. Vishal came back on the stage and asked everyone to get ready for the final round and smiled at me. The artists were ready with their kit, the top stylist were assigned to every model. They chose the perfect shades of lipstick and nail polish, mascara and what not. Fashion industry itself being beyond imagination, being perfect leads you a step ahead and one step missed will directly drop you at the bottom of the ladder. And if the confidence is broken, then there is no medicine to heal. Not everyone would find a best friend like Zara, nor everyone will wish for your goodwill, you simply can't trust anyone and so the journey gets challenging. Today was the peak, either stand there with pride or get down dropping to the start of life again.

I was heading to the dressing room when I saw Zed talking to someone, I reached to him, he saw me and introduced me to Prof Johnson Smith .

"I had worked with him for 2 years in US".

"Oh yeah you said", I said hello and extended my hand and introduced myself.

"I am Kanishka" and then Mr Smith bursted out laughing. I looked puzzled.

"Who doesn't know you?" and I blushed at his

statement.

"But sir how come you are here?".

"The car which would be gifted to winner is the latest invention by Zed", he said proudly and my eyes grew bigger.

"This came as a big surprise. I would die with all these surprises today", I said and laughed, then from behind Zara called me. I quickly excused myself. They both wished me all the best before leaving with utmost excitement. I narrated the entire thing to Zara in one breath.

"How lucky I am", I said and suddenly coughed badly and then it turned really ugly. Zara was worried, offered me water. We smiled.

Zara's face was worried but I always assured her everything was fine and was always supportive. The final ramp walk and I did not care about winning or losing. I laughed stupidly. The diva title would be for any one lucky girl, I kept talking in all excited tone and Zara tried to calm me both of us were eventually happy and wished each other for the best.

I then applied make up and changed to dark blue strapless and layered gown perfectly fitting my body, 6 inch heel, now was all set for the walk. The eight contestants gave their final walk, and now it was my turn. I stepped on the stage when Vishal announced my name I smiled at everyone and saw my parents and passed a big smile. My heart beat million times a second. As I was about to walk, my eyes filled with tears and slowly as I took a step ahead my eyes went completely blurred again. I thought I would collapse. It felt as if someone has stabbed a knife in my back. I could not see anything and did not let my broken confidence resemble in my walk. Panic struck me. I did not want to make fool out of myself in front of huge crowd. I quickly remembered Zed's joke, 10 steps straight and 5 steps right and as always I plastered a very natural and beautiful smile. I kept counting steps and as I took perfect 5 steps towards the right as well, I posed for pictures moving in left and right sides flaunting my curves and looking straight. No one would ever know what pain I was going through. I could not see anything. Just blurry vision filled my eyes.

I took similar steps back and then the IQ test. Literally freaked out. I was asked few questions and simply followed the voice answering smartly. I could not let my parents down. I did not want them to feel ashamed. I bowed down and took careful steps so that I didn't miss a step. As I headed towards backstage I fell down and Zara immediately helped me.

"Zara Zara....", I called her name out. I was immediately taken to the room, Zara knew something like this would happen. Zara was with me when Vishal announced her name on the stage. She did not give a damn, she looked for the bottle and sprinkled water on my face and after rubbing my eyes for several times I could finally see Zara and then Vishal announced her name again and I asked her to go but she did not pay attention instead she was worried about me and looked at my eyes keenly analyzing the problem, on the other hand I was yelling at her to go on the stage and finally Vishal announced that she was disqualified.

Zed and mom were completely taken aback, even they loved Zara. She immediately bought an ointment and eye drops, few drops which I did not care to even ask.

"Zara I am fine" I said but even I knew I was lying. "Oh really?! Congratulation", she said sarcastically. Finally all the models were on stage to hear the name of the winner. It was really a tough competition. So the jury announced... Well as you all are well aware about the judging criteria, 40% for overall marketability, 40% for the physique and 20% for the stage presence. And the winner of Femina miss India is..." a long pause and the crowd cheered and I bet all the nine participant's heart might have stopped breathing ot rather quick as mine

"The winner is Kanishka Mathur". And I was Dumbstruck. .

I stepped forward, bow down to all and saw my parents, Zed all happy. I blew a kiss at them. The crown was on my head now.

The much awaited day. There were goose bumps all over my body. Shiver ran down my spine.

A cheque of 50 lakhs was handed over by one of the jury members, and the car named NZ2606, was most special for me. They announced the Paris trip as an honor. I was so happy. Bouquets were presented and flowers showered on the podium. Red petals all over the stage with glitters.

Other participants congratulated me and met my parents and Zed at backstage. I made it I said and they hugged me one by one. Zara gave me a tight hug and she was super happy. After the late night party and lots of publicity, it was expected that I would be on the front page tomorrow. We all reached our private hotel in the morning and I quickly dozed off. Zara on the other side. We all were damn tired. A very peaceful night.

At around 1, in the noon when I woke up, I heard Zara talking over the phone, may be her dad as she happily narrated my victory and when I tried to look at the side from where her voice was coming I could see nothing. My eyes refused to show the image. I had a feeling of throwing up and so I called Zara, she came closer and I asked her to take me to washroom as I felt like vomiting. I splashed water over my face and rubbed like always but no sign of good vision. I called Zara and asked why I was not able to see anything. By her tone I could say she was worried. She called my parents and suggested to go for hospital.

Chapter Nineteen
At the Hospital

* * *

"I just hope I am wrong", Zara said under her breath in the hospital and that's when Zed looked at her and she was shocked that he heard.

"What do you mean?", He asked.

"Umm nothing", she said, then the doctor asked her parents to come along. He wanted to talk and so Zara too joined. She introduced herself as a doctor and the doctor clearly explained her everything.

"What I was worrying for, has come true", Zara said and let a tear fall out her eyes. Her parents were damn worried and then Zara explained to them clearly, very clearly.

She took a long breath before opening her mouth. "I have gone through her medical reports, the accident and the damages which haven't yet healed. She was not perfectly cured and then, now this. It's Fuch's dystrophy. In medical terms it's a progressive disease which affects only the eye, the cornea, and the round dome covering the iris leading to reduce specific cells and hence the vision is just not clear.

"What you mean Zara, is she blind now??", her mom asked.

Zara was quiet, her eyes spoke words, "just listen to me carefully", batting her eyes several times to avoid the flow of tears, she said without looking at her and voice full of shiver.

"This disease is somewhat more common in women and usually affects in their 50's and 60's. But here, in her case it appeared in adulthood due to the previous incident. The reports clearly state, she had bad injury on her head but it left 90% damaged cells within it by now. The nerves and cells connected to brain and eyes have been almost damaged… She stammered and continued, almost damaged leaving a very short time for her".

Her parents just looked at each other and were so shocked to hear. Earth swept from beneath their feet.

"What do you mean by short time", Zed asked, moving closer to Zara.

"Not more than 12 hours", she blurted out and looked at them while tears rolled down her cheeks. She could not face them and ran out of room trying to control her tears.

They were almost broken. It was very hard to believe the fact which left them devastated.

They entered the room altogether and saw her sleeping but in such a bad condition, all pipes inserted into her body, the saline and blood on either sides, the oxygen mask over her mouth made their heart wince in pain. The life support machines, the heart lung machine, tears rolled down. Zed left the room leaving her parents with her.

Zed called his parents and within no time they reached hospital, he burst out into tears. After four hours, she opened her eyes and looked at her parents who were sitting on the couch, her mom resting her head on her dad's chest, she was happy seeing them and called them. They hurriedly sat on either side of the bed. Tears rolled down, She removed the mask and tried to say something but was at loss of words. She simply smiled looking at them.

"Thank you princess ", her father said holding her mom's hand.

"Best gift", She said in a low voice. Almost a whisper.

"Pastry, apple cake pastry", she said in a low shrill voice.

"You wanna have pastry" her father asked and She nodded.

He smiled and left the room, he did not wish to leave her for a second also but, her wish was more important than anything as of now.

Her mom hugged her and simply cried holding her hand whispering sweet words in her ear, kissing her all over her face.

She was at loss of words, didn't have courage to look into her eyes. Indeed, Nishk wanted that moment to be like that forever, like she already knew what's going to happen with her.. She would never imagine going away from her parents. No such word exist where the bond between mom-dad relations could be explained. There was utmost peaceful yet scared silence.

Zara entered and they forced smiled. She held her hand and tears rolled down her cheeks. Nobody looked at her eyes. They all were stealing glances.

"My best friend", she said and kissed Zara's hand. She could not speak much. Her dad was back with pastry and they fed her with love, fear, fear of not having another such moment ever. His hands were terribly shaking. Even in such a worse time, she plastered a smile, creating lively atmosphere, very well aware as what was going to happen next. The time was actually running and this time her intuition was asking for her love. All of a sudden, at the peak time, she realized how much she loved him and did not wish to close eyes before seeing him for one last time and then she finally asked for Zed. Zed entered the room while all others left. Her mom kissed her before leaving and still tears running down her eyes.

Now just two of them in an awkward silence where the machine was creating a horrible background music.

Breaking the silence, Zed asked "How are you Nishk" , avoiding eye contact.

"I am fine, playing badminton wanna join", she said and both laughed.

He fought really hard not to go weak before her. He held her hand gently, rubbing his thumb on back of her hand gently.

He smiled, a very simple smile.

"Ok pay attention I have something to tell you".

She smiled and blinked her eye to continue.

By now she was trying hard to have a clear picture of him but she was able to see him.

He gently took her warm hand in his cold ones, due to the tension running in the back of his mind,sat on his knee and said, "Hey Kanishka Mathur", there was a clear creek in his voice, as he had cried for hours, which is very obvious "when I saw you the very first time, when we were nine, it was then that I fell for you. And as we grew older my love deepened like an ocean, I kept drowning and wanted to hold your hand long back but was waiting for the right time. To confess, it really needs lots of courage, I never felt like this for any other girl, you always made me special, an average looking guy, , a tear ran down his cheek, "Your simple touch would give me tickling sensation , a feather like touch, so soft,....and .... I am here proposing to you. You always being my dream girl", a long pause..... "I love you"....long pause and shiver in voice...... "Will you marry me?", He concluded and brought a ring out to her level and waited for her to reply.

She smiled brightly, nodded and said "yes". She was happy that he finally made it. But not many words came out of her mouth. He drew closer to her, taking care of every inch and hugged her. She slowly circled her arms around his neck, they hugged each other. He then slipped the ring in her finger, starring at each other, which felt like eternity and brought his lips closer to her. As their lips met, she responded with utmost passion, he placed one hand on her side waist and other caressing her hair, she cupped his face, and deepened the kiss. They gasped for breathe and moved forward touching their forehead, smiled looking at each other. She gave him a letter, pulling out from her pocket and hugged him again. She batted her eyes several times to stop the tears from flowing.

"I love you", she said after long pauses after each word. She raised her shivering hand and ran fingers through his hair lightly, then to his jaw, feeling every inch of him so closely for the last time.

Kissed his forehead. Touched his lips with her fingers, he kissed her palm.

She smiled.

"I love you", she said and hugged him again.. She repeated "I love you .....I love you too he responded. I am so happy, you accepted. I am so lucky to have you". He kept blabbering and then was a silence. He noticed the machines indicated something which was not normal. He was really scared. He placed her gently on bed and rushed to the doctor. Zara and the doctor came in and looked at each other clearly declaring her dead without uttering a word and hung their head down. No words were exchanged at all. The silence was not just for that moment or hour or day or year, the silence was forever. Not just she was gone, everything else disappeared in thin air. It all payed off at the end. Silence filled the room. A horrible silence filled in the lives connected to Kaniska Mathur.

Epilogue

I carried her body in my arms walking out of the room she weighed nothing. She always wanted me to carry her in bridal style with her hands around my neck. We reached the place few kilometers away followed by her family and close friends. The sticks were arranged and the rituals were performed. She was laid on the bed made of bamboo sticks where only her delicate body could perfectly fit in. Tears rolled down seeing her. I gently lifted her and placed her on the strand of wooden sticks and turned around. Her mom cried her heart out loud enough for her soul to hear and her dad caressing her. My heart forgot to beat. My whole world came crashing down to see all that happening right in front of my eyes. I kissed her gently on her forehead and closed my eyes tightly letting the tears to flow down. Her father took the flam beau and set those sticks on blaze and within a fraction of seconds the wood caught fire and I stood there still not knowing what to do. Helplessly till my love turned into ashes. Her words echoed in my mind, I felt my heart was made of paper, caught fire on its own leaving ashes behind. The suffocation made me carved for breath. Her body was nowhere physically available but her cheerful voice echoed my ear.

Everyone prayed for her body would heal and rejuvenate itself. But it was just a black day.

It set bar for what true love really is! Love of your love, love of your best friend, and not to forget love of parents.

We never know the reason for our birth, while we become the reason for others lives. Isn't this the biggest achievement?

Kanishka's life was deeply connected with her parents, they decided to be happy together until their last breath, not letting her efforts go in vain, missing her every single day. It was not easy for Zed as well, he would get himself so busy with work and traveling around, the void was just so deep. But he did not move on. He was no where mentally stable. Though he would frequently visit her parents, but his inner peace was long lost. Zara went home with a heavy heart. The pain and experience shattered her. She decided to never come back to India.

Dear readers,

Thank you for choosing this book hope was up to your expectations.

I, being little off track from the techie world, would love your response by letters.

Practicing ancient methods making my routine life little interesting and I promise to write back, feel free to ask your questions or give any suggestions.

I would appreciate your extreme steps out of your busy schedule which will ultimately motivate me to write many more.

Kindly drop your letters at : { G-120, Sushant Lok III Sector 57 Gurgaon-122001 }

You can also write back on: swaraliwankhade@gmail.com or follow up http://disjointdestinies.blogspot.in/

Love you all!

